Touching the Waves

"So you think Rosie might be with Apollo?" Lauren asked.

Jody nodded, gazing sympathetically into Lauren's worried face.

"Here comes another one," Brittany called out. "Look, Lauren, is that Rosie?"

Lauren turned eagerly back to look, shading her eyes against the sun. Almost immediately, she shook her head.

But Jody recognized the solitary dolphin. "It's Apollo!" she cried joyfully.

In response, Apollo reared up out of the water, clicking and chattering urgently.

"It's almost like he's trying to tell you something," said Janet Davis in surprise.

Look out for more titles in this series

Dolphin Diaries™

Ben M. Baglio

Illustrations by Judith Lawton

TOUCHING THE WAVES

AN
APPLE
PAPERBACK

SCHOLASTIC INC.
New York Toronto London Auckland Sydney
Mexico City New Delhi Hong Kong Buenos Aires

No part of this publication may be reproduced in whole or in part, or stored in a retrieval system, or transmitted in any form or by any means, electronic, mechanical, photocopying, recording, or otherwise, without written permission of the publisher. For information regarding permission, write to Working Partners Limited, 1 Albion Place, London W6 OQT United Kingdom.

ISBN 0-439-31948-X

All rights reserved. Published by Scholastic Inc., 555 Broadway, New York, NY 10012, by arrangement with Working Partners Limited. DOLPHIN DIARIES is a trademark of Working Partners Limited. SCHOLASTIC, APPLE PAPERBACKS, and associated logos are trademarks and/or registered trademarks of Scholastic Inc.

24 23 22 21 20 19 18 17 16 15   6 7 8 9/0

Printed in the U.S.A.   40
First Scholastic printing, October 2001

Special thanks to Lisa Tuttle

Thanks also to Dr. Horace Dobbs at
International Dolphin Watch for reviewing the
information contained in this book

1

June 25 — after breakfast.

Apollo and the other dolphins stayed around Dolphin Dreamer with us all through the night, and now it looks like they are headed for Key West, too! I can't help feeling that Apollo doesn't want to say good-bye any more than I do. Maybe he is hoping, just like me, that we'll get another chance to swim together.

Dr. Taylor calls this "fantasy," but I know there is a special bond between me and Apollo. After all, he can't explain why else this group of dolphins should be traveling *so closely with* Dolphin Dreamer, *and even he has to admit that dolphins are very intelligent. He just muttered something about "coincidence." But what does he know? He was never in the water with Apollo; never touched him, never gazed into his eyes, never felt that magical, peaceful feeling. . . . It's hard to find the right words for how being with Apollo makes me feel. It's so special. . . .*

Jody McGrath sighed dreamily and closed her diary, thinking about the magical events of the past few days. Barely a week ago she, her family, and the rest of the crew of *Dolphin Dreamer* had sailed out of Fort Lauderdale, Florida, to embark on an international research project on dolphins. Since then, the dolphin she'd named Apollo had saved her life, and now he and his friends were swimming alongside the boat like a guard of honor.

She was suddenly eager to see him again. Stowing diary and pen safely away, she rolled off her bunk and left the cabin.

Jody found her parents with their assistant, Maddie, at one of the computers in the main cabin, going over some data. Dr. Jefferson Taylor seemed to be working hard on his own laptop, but as she walked past, Jody saw the bright colors of a deck of playing cards laid out on his screen and realized he was just playing a game of solitaire!

She smiled to herself. Dolphin Universe had been Craig and Gina McGrath's idea, but they had found it difficult to raise enough money for the project. Then PetroCo, a large oil company, had offered to provide the rest of the money needed to make Dolphin Universe possible — but only if one of their own scientists, Dr. Jefferson Taylor, was added to the crew. So far, however, no one had worked out what use Dr. Taylor was going to be!

Jody walked through the main cabin without disturbing anyone, just exchanging a quick smile with her mother. She poked her head into the galley, where Mei Lin, the boat's cook and engineer, was washing the dishes from breakfast. "Are there any of those yummy rolls left?" she asked.

Mei Lin smiled. "For you, Jody, I think I can find one."

"Thanks!" Jody bit gratefully into the sweet, soft

dough. She was still eating as she swung up through the hatch and out onto the deck.

Harry Pierce, the boat's captain, was at the helm, while his second mate, the handsome Cameron Tucker, was checking the sails. Jody's younger brothers, twins Sean and Jimmy, were close at hand, listening attentively while Harry explained something about wind direction and speed. Brittany, Harry's daughter, was sitting nearby, but she had her back to the others as she stared out to sea with a frown on her face.

Dolphin Dreamer was flying along. Jody gazed up at the cloudless blue sky and breathed in the salty air. It was going to be another blazingly hot day, but for the moment at least, the winds were strong. She heard Cam say that at this rate they'd make Key West in under two hours.

"Thank goodness!" said Brittany loudly. "I can't wait to get to Key West."

"Oh? Is Key West a favorite place, Britt?" Sounding interested, Cam turned his sparkling green eyes in her direction.

Brittany tossed her head, sending her long hair flying. "I prefer Miami or Palm Beach, actually," she said loudly. "But anywhere with shops and people and things to do has got to be better than being stuck on this boat in the middle of nowhere!"

Jody saw Harry Pierce wince at his daughter's words. She felt sorry for him. Brittany had been a last-minute, and most unwilling, addition to the crew of *Dolphin Dreamer*. Telling Brittany that her father would be taking her to the Bahamas for her summer vacation, her mother had dropped Brittany off on the day they were to sail, and then left the country! As there was no one else who could look after her, Brittany had been forced to come along. Harry was trying his best — they all were — to make Brittany feel welcome, but Jody had the feeling that nothing anyone could do would be good enough for her.

Jody climbed up to the forward deck and looked over the side. Her heart beat faster as she saw the dolphins racing along with the boat.

There were the seven wild bottle-nosed dolphins: Apollo, Artemis, Poseidon, Hermes, Triton, Castor, and Pollux. They were leaping through the water, pushing and jostling one another for the best position, "bow-riding" one after another on the wave created by the forward movement of the boat. Dolphins loved to do this with boats of all sizes. Jody's dad had told her that dolphins had even been spotted riding the wave created by the head of a large whale.

Jody felt a big smile break out across her face as she watched them. Her spirits lifted as effortlessly as the dolphins leaped and dived. It was almost impossible not to feel happy in the presence of these beautiful creatures. The bad atmosphere caused by Brittany seemed to blow away like sea foam in the wind.

Eventually, the dolphins grew tired of their sport with the boat and swam off, disappearing into the blue distance. Jody felt a pang as she watched them swim away, but somehow she felt certain this was not the last she'd see of them.

Cam, Craig, and Gina got to work taking down and stowing the sails as the buildings on the shores of Key West came into sight, and Harry switched on the engine.

Moments later Mei Lin appeared on deck. "Harry, I don't like the sound of that motor," she said, frowning slightly.

Jody couldn't hear anything unusual in the noisy drone, but she saw Harry listen intently and then nod slowly.

"Something's wrong," he agreed. "Luckily, for the next two weeks we won't have anything else to do, so we've got all the time we need to —"

"Nothing else to do!" Brittany whirled around to glare at her father. "What about taking me shopping, and sight-seeing? You *promised*."

Harry looked uncomfortable. He cleared his throat. "Of course I will, love."

"Don't worry. I was fixing engines single-handedly long before I met your father," Mei Lin said to Brittany, trying to lighten the mood. "I don't need him. I'll be glad for you to take him out of my hair!"

"Have a little more respect for your captain," Harry said with a mock scowl before turning back to his daughter. "There, you see? I can take a couple of days off. We'll do whatever you want." He smiled hopefully.

But Brittany's furious scowl did not relax. "A couple of days?" she repeated. "Out of two whole weeks? And we have to stay on the boat the *whole* of the rest of the time? What am I supposed to do with myself? Can't we go to a hotel?"

"Of course not," Harry replied, frowning himself now. "This is where I live, so it's where you live while you're with me."

Brittany turned and pointed a finger at Jody. "But *she* isn't going to stay on the boat! I know, because I heard her mother telling her to pack!"

Jody shook her head. Brittany really was spoiled and rude beyond belief! "If you'd bothered to listen, you'd know that we're not going off on a vacation to a hotel," she told the other girl. "We're going to visit CETA, on Cedar Key."

Brittany scowled. "See-ta," she repeated. "What's that?"

"C-E-T-A," Jody spelled out. She paused to make sure she remembered the name exactly and then went on. "It stands for 'Cetaceans as Educational and Therapeutic Associates.' Cetaceans are dolphins," she added, seeing the blank expression on Brittany's face.

Brittany made a face. "I might have known, dolphins again!" she groaned. "But you still haven't told me what it is."

"It's a special center for disabled children," Jody explained. "I think the kids get to swim with dolphins, and it helps them, somehow. I don't really know much more about it — that's what we're here to find out." She began to feel excited again, forgetting her irritation with Brittany as she thought of the days ahead. "It's run by an old friend of my mom's. Her name is Alice Rozakis, and her husband, Jerry, is a psychologist who specializes in helping children. And they've got a daughter my age named Lauren. Gosh, it must be so great for her, to live in a place like that!"

"Only if she likes dolphins," Brittany muttered.

Jody knew that Brittany had no interest in dolphins, so she could hardly believe her ears when the other girl turned to her father and declared, "I want to go to . . . er . . . CETA as well."

Harry frowned. "Brittany, you can't just invite yourself —"

Another voice interrupted him. "We'd love to have Brittany join us, Harry."

Jody turned in surprise at her father's voice. Craig and Gina had come out on deck and must have heard the conversation.

"I'll just give Alice a call on the cell phone, to make sure there's room for one more," added Gina, moving briskly toward the hatch.

Jody turned back to Brittany. "But — but you don't even like dolphins!" she protested. She'd had to put up with the bad-tempered girl for long enough and was looking forward to a break. "You'd enjoy yourself much more here in Key West — your dad said he'll take you out."

Brittany shrugged her shoulders moodily. "Yeah, for two whole days. If I have to spend the rest of the time on this boat I'll go crazy," she said in a low voice. "Anyway, there's got to be more to do than just look at dolphins on Cedar Key."

Gina poked her head out of the hatch. "Alice says the

more the merrier! Plenty of room in her big minivan, and it'll be like a slumber party in Lauren's bedroom. Lauren's looking forward to it."

Jody's heart sank. Desperately, she tried again to change Brittany's mind. "But we won't have time for sight-seeing — it'll be dolphins, dolphins, dolphins all the time. And you'll be stuck if you come with us — you won't get to do anything fun with your dad!"

"Of course she will," said Gina, giving Jody a warning look. "Harry, Alice says there's an anchorage by their house on Cedar Key, so after you've finished your re-pairs and so on, you can join us there. And of course we can bring Brittany back here anytime. Alice says they come down to Key West every few days to shop — they're only about twenty miles up the high-way."

Harry nodded. "All right. That's very kind. . . . Thank you," he said quietly, looking from Gina to Craig before nodding at his daughter. "Okay, Brittany, run and pack a few things if you're going."

A triumphant smile spread across Brittany's face. She hurried below without another word.

"Don't bother to say thank you," Jody muttered. She stared at the rows of moored boats they were chugging past. She felt as if a heavy weight had settled on her shoulders.

Sean and Jimmy were the first off the boat once it docked, challenging each other to races and acting like puppies let out of a cage.

Dr. Taylor was the next to leave. He wasn't going to Cedar Key. He'd made his own arrangements to visit some other research projects in the Florida Keys. "I will, of course, supply you with detailed reports, so you won't miss anything," he told Jody's parents as he left.

"Thank you. I'm sure that will be very useful to the project," said Gina politely.

They watched from the deck, waving, as Dr. Taylor drove away in a rental car.

Craig McGrath gave a gusty sigh. "Whew, I'm looking forward to a vacation from that guy!"

Jody was also rather relieved to have a break from Dr. Taylor's rather stuffy presence. If only she could have a break from Brittany, too!

Gina McGrath shook her head, smiling. "He's harmless enough," she said. "And he probably feels the same way about us!" She picked up her bag. "Come on, we might as well get going — Alice said she'd meet us in the parking lot, by the flagpole."

Jody shrugged on her backpack. She'd packed lightly, just a few clothes, her diary, and the book she was reading. Since Cedar Key was not far from Key West, they could easily return to *Dolphin Dreamer* whenever they liked.

As she followed her parents and Maddie along the jetty, Jody found her legs were a bit wobbly. Solid ground felt strange beneath her feet after a few days at sea.

"Gina! Over here!"

The call came from a tall, fair-haired woman waving her arms vigorously above her head.

Gina McGrath broke into a smile and rushed forward. "Alice!" The two women hugged each other warmly.

"You remember Craig, of course," Gina said, stepping back with a smile.

"I think the last time we met was at your wedding,"

13

said the tall woman, shaking Craig's hand. Her face was tanned and friendly and her smile was warm.

"This is our daughter, Jody, and our two sons, Sean and Jimmy," Gina went on. "Brittany Pierce, the daughter of our captain. And this is Maddie, our invaluable assistant — I think you've exchanged a few e-mails with her already!"

They all smiled and nodded at one another, and then Alice Rozakis led them to her vehicle where a tall, serious-looking girl with her brown hair tied back in a long braid was waiting. "This is my daughter, Lauren," she said. Lauren smiled and gave a brief wave at the others.

"Now let's get out of this heat and on our way!" Alice suggested, linking an arm through Gina's.

Jody'd hoped to talk to Lauren — she had about a million questions to ask her — but somehow, as they all piled in, Brittany managed to grab the seat next to Lauren, and Jody had to squash in with her brothers. She tried not to mind as she watched Brittany chatting away with Lauren, but she couldn't help feeling left out.

Instead of asking Lauren about CETA, as Jody would have done, Brittany quizzed her about her favorite movies, TV shows, and pop groups. They seemed to like all the same ones.

Jody gazed out of the window at the ocean, which glittered in the sun on either side of Highway 1. Even now, she seemed to feel its movement beneath her. Soon they left the highway for the entrance to CETA, and Jody sat up, alert.

The center turned out to be a group of low, white-washed buildings with red-tiled roofs in the Spanish style. The Rozakis family home was right next door to the CETA office, and they shared a big, walled court-yard facing out to sea.

As she showed them around, Alice explained that the center had been built around a natural lagoon. This had been fenced off from the open sea to create a large "sea pen" for the resident dolphins. Connected to this big "pen" by canals that could be left open or fenced off, were two large pools, one of them very shallow. This was for the benefit of children who couldn't swim or weren't comfortable in deep water. The bigger pool had a wooden dock projecting out into it.

A short, dark-bearded man in swimming trunks was

standing on the dock with a slim young woman and a little boy who also wore trunks and a life jacket.

"That's my dad," Lauren said proudly.

"Jerry's working right now," Alice explained. "He's promised to join us as soon as he can. Let me just pop into the office and see if there are any messages."

Everyone followed her into the office, which was an airy, friendly space with bright yellow walls, decorated with children's colorful drawings. A young woman with long, shining black hair was seated at one of the two desks, typing something into a computer. She looked up with a welcoming smile.

Alice briefly introduced them. "This is Kim Lo, Jerry's assistant. She keeps everything organized for us. Any messages?" she asked.

"Six e-mails and two phone calls wanting information about the program," Kim replied. "All routine, don't worry — I can deal with them."

"Thank you," said Alice warmly. "I'm just going to get our guests settled, but give me a yell if you need anything."

Once inside the house, Craig and Gina went with Alice.

Lauren showed Sean and Jimmy to a twin-bedded guest room, then took Jody and Brittany to her own bedroom. "You guys can have the twin beds," she said, pointing. "There's an air mattress for me — don't worry, it's really comfortable."

Jody was interested to see that on one of Lauren's bedroom walls was the same poster of leaping dolphins that she had at home.

But before she could comment on it, Brittany called out, "Hey, Lauren, could I use your computer to check my e-mail?"

"Sure," said Lauren. "But maybe later? I wanted to introduce you to —"

"Please?" Brittany interrupted, smiling persuasively. "I'm expecting to hear from my mother — I really can't wait!"

Lauren shrugged. "Okay." She looked at Jody. "How about you? Want to come meet the teachers?"

Jody thought she'd rather meet the dolphins, but she

wanted to be polite, so she nodded. "But shouldn't we wait for Mom and Dad, and Maddie?"

"Oh, my folks'll give 'em the grand tour after they've finished gossiping and drinking coffee. Why should we wait? Come and get introduced!" Lauren's gray eyes gleamed with excitement.

"Okay." Jody wondered what the big deal was about the teachers. Could Lauren have a crush on one of them? "How many teachers are there?" she asked, gazing at Lauren's long, brown braid as she followed her through the house.

"Just four," Lauren replied. "We'd like to have more, but well, it takes a very special type to relate well to the kids who come here for help, and not everyone can do it."

Instead of turning toward the buildings when they came out of the house, Lauren walked toward the lagoon. Jody immediately became more interested: Maybe the teachers were in the water with the dolphins and the children?

Yet she couldn't see anyone as they drew near. The figures who had been standing on the dock were now gone, the shallow pool was empty, and she couldn't see anyone but Lauren and herself in the whole area.

Lauren led the way onto a wooden dock, which curved along beside the fence that separated the lagoon from the open sea. She gazed out at the blue-green water for a moment, and then she whistled.

Jody looked at Lauren, impressed. The whistle was very much like a sound made by dolphins.

Seconds later, a sleek gray form came shooting through the water toward them, the familiar curved dorsal fin slicing through the surface.

Jody laughed with delight. "Oh, you teaser," she said to Lauren. "Making me think I was going to meet some boring old teachers . . ."

"But this *is* one of the CETA teachers," said Lauren, a look of utter innocence on her serious face. "The dolphins are the teachers here, because they're the ones who help the kids to learn. My dad thinks of himself as just an assistant — he'll tell you that."

The dolphin poked his head up out of the water and clacked and whistled at Lauren. Then he turned his head to examine Jody with a bright, intelligent eye.

"This is Nick," said Lauren. "See that little notch on his fin? That'll help you to recognize him."

Another bottle-nosed dolphin popped up beside Nick, whistling.

"Hi, Nora," Lauren said. She whistled back, setting off a chorus of whistles from the two dolphins. "Nick, Nora, meet Jody. Can you whistle, Jody?" They like it when you do."

It was hard to stop smiling at the enchanting crea-

Two of CETA's teachers — Nick and Nora!

tures long enough to pucker up, but Jody did her best. She was rewarded with a stream of chattering clicks and whistles from both Nick and Nora, who rose out of the water to nod their heads, as if in approval.

"I have a recorder," Jody told Lauren. "The dolphins we've met at sea seemed to love me playing it to them. I wish I hadn't left it on the boat."

Lauren nodded. "The dolphins love music," she said. "When Dad sits out in the courtyard playing his guitar, they all come into the shallow pool to listen! You could pick up your recorder later." She looked around. "Maxi's over there, so Rosie must be nearby. Rosie is Maxi's daughter."

They walked farther along the dock to meet the other two dolphins.

Maxi was the biggest and, Lauren said, the oldest of the CETA dolphins. She seemed uninterested in her visitors, or maybe she'd just had a hard day. She swam slowly away as Rosie came speeding up to check them out. Rosie was a slim, sleek young thing with a knot of scar tissue over one eye.

"What happened?" Jody asked, pointing.

21

"Fish hook," Lauren said solemnly. "The vet said if it had gone in one inch nearer, she'd have lost the eye."

Jody shuddered. "How awful!"

But the accident was obviously long forgotten by Rosie, who leaped straight out of the water when the girls drew near, showering them with water.

Jody gave a shriek and then laughed. Like an echo, Rosie made a sound very much like human laughter.

"Rosie's our wild girl," said Lauren affectionately. "But only if you can take it. Put somebody shy or scared in the pool with her and she'll be as sweet as pie."

"She's your favorite, isn't she?" Jody guessed.

Lauren hesitated, then nodded. "I love them all," she said. "But I guess I do love Rosie the best. I've known her since she was a baby. She's only five now — that's a young teenager, Mom says."

Jody recognized a kindred spirit in Lauren. Here was someone else who knew the joys of having a dolphin for a friend. She grinned, suddenly sure that the next two weeks on Cedar Key were going to be absolutely wonderful.

2

Jody spent the rest of the afternoon being shown around by Lauren. Later, they were joined by Brittany and the twins. They didn't meet Lauren's father, Dr. Jerry Rozakis, until he appeared at the dinner table, apologizing for keeping everyone waiting.

"Call me Jerry," Dr. Rozakis said as he shook Jody's hand. "Everybody does." He was a short, wiry man with a head of black curls and piercing blue eyes. Although he was lively and enthusiastic, and obviously pleased to have guests, Jody thought he looked tired.

They were just finishing big bowls of fiery chili

served with tortillas and salad, when Bud, a tall, lanky young man who helped with the care of the dolphins, came in.

"Hey, Jerry? Sorry to bother you," he said, "but there's something going on down at the sea gates. They won't come in to be fed." Bud waved his big hands around. "I don't know what to do. . . . I know I'm not supposed to leave till they've had their dinner, but I don't want to be late for my date."

Jerry sighed and put his napkin on the table. "That's okay, you run along, Bud. I'll make sure they're fed."

"Thanks, Jerry. Appreciate it!" Bud said, and hurried out of the door.

Jody saw that Alice didn't look pleased. "Really, Jerry, you're too easygoing. We pay him to do a job — he knew the hours when he took it," she said disapprovingly.

"I don't mind, honey," Jerry replied, rubbing his face wearily as he spoke. "You know I like to check on them every night myself."

"Is there a problem?" Gina asked, sounding concerned.

"Only with our assistant," said Alice, managing a smile. "The dolphins are probably not responding because they're too interested in something on the other side of the fence. Wild dolphins, most likely," she explained. "They stop by to have a chat with ours from time to time. Our dolphins get very excited. Well, they're social creatures. But after a while they'll remember it's feeding time. There wouldn't be a problem if Bud wasn't in such a hurry."

Wild dolphins! Jody caught her breath.

"We've been swimming with wild dolphins," Sean said proudly.

"Can we go and look?" Lauren was eager, watching her mother for permission.

Alice nodded. "If you've finished your dinner," she replied.

"Come on Jody, Brittany," Lauren said. She looked at her mother. "We can feed them, then Dad can just relax."

"He can try," said Alice with a short laugh. She smiled at her daughter. "Thank you, Lauren. That would be helpful."

25

The twins, too, were scrambling out of their seats. Jody expected Brittany to make a scornful comment about dolphins. She never hesitated to sneer at Jody's interest, but she must have decided it was worth being nice to Lauren, because she followed without a word.

Outside, night had fallen. Jody couldn't see any of the dolphins in the dark water.

"Where are they?" Jimmy demanded.

"Shh. Listen," Lauren whispered.

The sound of distant creaks, clicks, and whistles carried on the breeze over the water.

Jody's heart began to pound. The hairs on the back of her neck lifted at the sound of one particular, strangely familiar, whistle. "Apollo," she whispered.

"What?" Brittany snapped. "How do you know? You can't even see them! It could be any dolphin!"

But Jody was sure. "It's him. That was his signature whistle — I recognize it!"

"As if you could recognize a whistle!" Brittany said scornfully.

"Every dolphin makes a special whistle, which might be like a human's name," Lauren said, gently backing

26

up Jody. "It's called a 'signature' whistle because it seems to be the way dolphins identify themselves. I've learned to tell the difference between the sounds our dolphins make — there! That was Rosie!"

"This is boring," Jimmy complained. "I can't see a thing! I thought we were going to get to feed the dolphins."

"Yes, we are," Lauren said. "They might be ready to come now." She walked over to the side of the water where two big white buckets full of fish had been left, along with a large whistle hanging on a thick cord. She picked this up and blew a long blast on it.

After a long moment of silence, two dark, snub-nosed shapes popped up from the water, practically at Lauren's feet. Everyone except Lauren jumped.

"They're so fast and quiet," Brittany said. "I didn't even hear them coming."

She sounded nervous rather than admiring, Jody thought.

"Yeah, aren't they great?" Lauren replied. As she spoke, Lauren tossed two fish out. "Here, you want to feed them?" she asked, turning to Brittany.

Brittany backed away. "No thanks. I don't want to get my hands all smelly."

"I do!" Sean and Jimmy spoke at once, and jostled each other to get at the fish.

"Take it easy," Lauren said, laughing. "Even dolphins don't fight over dead fish! There's plenty to go around."

"But only two dolphins," Sean noted. "Which oncs are these?"

"Nick and Nora," Lauren replied. "They're the greediest. Maxi and Rosie will be here in a minute."

Sure enough, seconds later, another dolphin glided up to be fed. Jody identified her by her size as Maxi. "I guess Rosie must still be gossiping with Apollo," she said.

Brittany snorted. "That is so babyish — as if animals could talk!"

"My mom thinks they do," Lauren said calmly, still flinging fish into the gaping mouths below her. "Maybe they don't use words, like us, but they do tell each other things. Mom worked on a study about it years ago."

"Oh," Brittany said, sounding surprised. "So what are they telling each other now?"

Lauren shrugged. "I wish I knew. Mom says maybe the wild dolphins come to find out if the dolphins behind the fence are okay, to find out if they're mistreated, or prisoners. If that's true, I hope ours are telling the wild ones that they're happy here."

"But they *are* prisoners here, aren't they?" Brittany challenged. "You've got them trapped behind that fence."

Jody was eager to hear Lauren's reply. She'd wondered uneasily about this herself.

"No," said Lauren. "They don't have to stay here if they don't want to. There's a gate in that fence — the sea gate. We open it every weekend and they can go out if they want. But so far, they've always come back. They must like it here."

Jody gazed into the distance at the dark sea, where Apollo and his friends were on the other side of the fence. Although she couldn't see it now, she recalled that the fence rose only a couple of yards above the surface of the water. A dolphin could easily jump that high. That meant that the CETA dolphins could escape out to sea at anytime, whether the sea gates were open or not. They must stay because they liked it here, as Lauren said.

"Hmm, so they're kind of like your pets," Brittany said. "I had a cat called Hazel who used to go off wandering for hours — sometimes all day. But she always came back at dinnertime. Until —" She broke off.

"What happened?" Lauren asked gently.

Brittany shrugged. "We never found out. My mother said she probably found a new home she liked better. . . . But I think she must have died. She probably got hit by a car. . . ." Brittany's voice sounded flat and sad.

How awful, Jody thought, feeling sorry for the poor lost cat. She was surprised to find that she also felt sorry for Brittany.

"Gosh, you must miss her," said Lauren warmly.

Brittany nodded a little stiffly, but let Lauren put a comforting arm around her.

They carried on feeding the dolphins together,

Lauren still fussing around Brittany. But it was clear from the way that Brittany ignored Jody that she wanted no sympathy from her.

When feeding time was over, Jody left Brittany and Lauren to it and, feeling a little lonely, went to rejoin the others inside the house.

June 26 — after breakfast.
Lauren is taking tennis lessons this summer, and her mom arranged for me, Sean, and Jimmy to have lessons this week, too. Of course, she didn't know Brittany would be with us . . . I earned lots of brownie points by saying Brittany could take my place and I would stay here. The truth is, I'd much rather stay here and learn how "dolphin-assisted therapy" works, instead of standing in the hot sun trying to hit a ball over a net.

Even so, I didn't much like being left behind. I got a funny feeling in my stomach, watching Lauren and Brittany go off for their first lesson together, a few minutes ago. They were giggling about something, and hardly seemed to notice when I said good-bye. It really hurt!

I like Lauren, and I think she likes me. We both love dolphins more than anything, and I'm sure we'd be better friends if Brittany wasn't here.

But Brittany is making a real effort to get all of Lauren's attention. She doesn't let on to Lauren that, really, she couldn't care less about dolphins — she just changes the subject — to things I don't know much about, like pop music, fashion, and some TV shows they both love which I've never seen. Plus, she's got Lauren feeling sorry for her, and pretends to be this sweet, misunderstood girl that everybody else is mean to (especially me!).

Well, I am not going to stoop to Brittany's level. I won't say anything bad about her to Lauren — but I can write down how I really feel here, where no one else will see it.

The working day at CETA was about to begin. Craig and Gina had decided that, with the parents' permission, they would make a video record of each session, to become part of the Dolphin Universe database.

As they set up their equipment, Jerry Rozakis filled them in. "Our first patient of the day is named Heather. She's four, and has Down's syndrome." He bent down to stroke Maxi, who was lying quietly in the shallow pool, then went on seriously, "Long ago, it was assumed that people born with Down's could never learn anything. But we know now that's not true. Some people are more severely handicapped than others, but you never really know how much someone can achieve unless you give them their best chance. Children like Heather need help in paying attention so they can begin to learn. And a good way to get someone's attention is to connect learning with something fun."

"Dolphins?" Jody guessed.

Jerry grinned. "Right. A grown-up like me is boring, but a dolphin is fun. So guess who's the best teacher here?"

Jody grinned back. "Maxi!" She liked Lauren's dad, and she bet he was a great teacher, whatever he said.

Jerry gazed out at the deeper water, where the other three dolphins dipped in and out of view. "Rosie, Nick, Nora . . . they're all wonderful teachers, too," he went on. "We try to match the personalities of the children to those of the dolphins. Maxi is the most 'motherly' — older than the others; the most patient. She's the best choice for younger or more timid children. Rowdier children might get on better with Rosie or Nick. And sometimes one of the dolphins will just take a special liking to a particular child. Dolphins know who they like —" He broke off as the door to the office opened.

His assistant, Kim, came out with a man and a woman who were holding the hands of a little girl in a red swimsuit and a bright orange life jacket. They were all smiling broadly.

"Guess what, Jerry," called the woman, who seemed to be the child's mother. "Heather got herself dressed this morning — she put on her swimsuit all by herself!"

"Wow, that's great!" Jerry crouched down to talk to the little girl. "Is that right, Heather? No help from anybody?"

"No help," Heather replied proudly. "I do it all by myself!"

"Well, you'll have to tell Maxi about it — I'm sure she'll be pleased with you," Jerry said.

Heather clapped her hands excitedly. "Want see Maxi! Want go in water!"

From the pool came a string of clicking sounds that

seemed to say Maxi was as eager for this meeting as Heather was.

"Soon," Jerry promised. "First, we're going to sit on the side of the pool, and you and Maxi are going to play a game with me, okay?"

Heather nodded, and sat down obediently.

Jerry showed her a box of brightly colored plastic toys. "Find the blue ball," he said.

The little girl plunged her hand into the box and grabbed a blue ring.

"No, listen to *both* words, Heather: blue . . . ball." Jerry spoke slowly and clearly.

This time, Heather paused, and looked carefully before pulling out the correct toy.

"Yes! Very good, Heather!" Jerry smiled as he praised, and offered a reward. "Would you like to throw the blue ball to Maxi?"

"Yes!" Heather beamed with delight. She drew her arm back and threw the ball. A moment later, Maxi returned it to her, which caused Heather to laugh and clap her hands.

Maxi at work!

"Okay, Heather, now I want you to find a red block," said Jerry.

The little girl found it the first time.

The simple lesson went on for about ten minutes, and then Heather was allowed to slip into the pool along with Jerry, to play with Maxi. Although this was her reward for paying attention and doing well, the lesson wasn't over. Kim tossed different colored rings into the water, then Maxi fetched them, one at a time, and returned them to Heather, who had to name the color for Jerry. She got them right every time, without pausing or struggling.

Jody watched, fascinated. She knew that some people — even her scientist mother — scoffed at people who made unscientific claims for dolphins having special powers. But it seemed that there was something almost magical between this little girl and Maxi.

When Heather's time was up, Jerry rejoined the McGraths while Kim went to fetch the next patient from the office.

Jerry explained that ten-year-old Bobby Fox was severely mentally retarded. He couldn't even speak, and the doctors and teachers who had tested him didn't know how much he could understand.

"His parents had nearly given up hope of ever reaching him," said Jerry in a low voice. "But in the weeks that he's been coming here, we've seen a great improvement. It won't mean as much to you since you didn't see him a month ago, but we think of him as one of our great successes."

A few minutes later, Kim returned with a dark-haired woman wearing a long blue dress, and a short, dark-haired boy in swimming trunks and a life jacket. He dashed toward the deeper pool, where Jody had noticed Nora swimming by herself. The woman cried out and tried to grab him, but he was already out of her reach.

"Bobby, stop!" Jerry spoke loudly and firmly, and the boy froze at the edge of the pool.

Nora poked her nose up out of the water and made a sound like a creaking hinge.

At this, the boy began to make a clicking sound.

Jody caught her breath in surprise. Jerry had said that Bobby couldn't speak, but here he was trying his best to talk — with a dolphin!

The first part of Bobby's session took place on the dock overlooking the deeper pool. Jerry used the same box of toys, and asked the same sort of questions that he had asked of Heather. But what the four-year-old had found easy was a great struggle for this ten-year-old.

Jody could see that Bobby had trouble understanding even simple ideas such as "bigger" and "smaller." It was very hard for him to sort bricks by color and size. But he tried. He made noises of frustration and anger, but he did not give up. Jody saw that he was so eager for a chance to join Nora in the water that he would do his best to do what he was asked.

After ten minutes of this hard work, Bobby was allowed to get into the water with Nora. She swam right up to him, and Bobby stroked her gently, gazing at her lovingly. Jody felt a lump in her throat as she remembered Apollo. She knew just how Bobby felt.

3

Alice returned with Lauren, Brittany, Sean, and Jimmy at noon, when everyone stopped work for a quick lunch of sandwiches and salad.

"So what do you think of CETA so far?" Alice asked Gina and Craig as they gathered in the big kitchen to eat.

"It's very impressive," Craig replied. "I do have some questions, though."

"Fire away," said Jerry, biting into a cheese and tomato sandwich.

"Well, I understand the theory behind it," Craig began slowly. "And it's clear from what we've seen this morning that dolphin-assisted therapy really does work for the children, but what's going to happen after they leave? They're making progress while working with the dolphins, but there won't be any dolphins to help them out at home."

Jerry put down his sandwich and scratched his beard. "That's true. There is a limit to what we can do here. It wouldn't be practical for children to keep coming to us day after day, for years on end. We aren't aiming to replace other kinds of schools or therapies. But we hope that the experience of learning with dolphins for a little while will have a lasting effect. The idea is to 'jump-start' the child, give them an extra boost that will get them going."

Gina paused with her fork above her salad. "And does that work?" she asked.

"Yes, for many people," Jerry replied. "Sometimes it's enough for the kids to realize that they *can* learn — a breakthrough can lead to real progress that will continue long after they leave us."

"Did you meet Heather?" Alice asked from across the table.

Craig, Gina, Jody, and Maddie all nodded.

"Heather's a good example," Jerry said enthusiastically. "When her parents said she'd dressed herself this morning, I thought, *yes*! Her excitement about the dolphins has carried over into her daily life — she's just generally more alert. And that has lasting effect — it nearly always does. The more she learns to do, the more self-confidence that will give her, and the more she will try to do."

"I could see that Heather really loved being with Maxi," Jody said.

Her mother nodded. "The dolphins certainly kept the children's attention — which, as you said earlier, is the first step in getting someone to learn anything."

"I think you've convinced us all that dolphins are great teachers," Craig added.

"Oh, they're more than that," Alice told them. "They also play a great role as healers."

Jody leaned forward, even more curious now. But she saw that her mother was looking skeptical.

Gina shook her head. "Oh, Alice. You're not talking about all those people who go swimming with dolphins and claim they've been cured of their illnesses, are you?"

Alice gave her old friend a level look across the table. "Yes, Gina, I am."

"But that's just an emotional reaction," Gina protested. "It's not something you can measure, or prove. We're scientists, Alice — we have to look at the facts, not just listen to people's stories."

Craig cleared his throat. "Um, but, Gina, you know that, as a psychologist, Jerry does have to listen to people's stories, and be concerned with their emotions."

Jody recognized her father's peace-making tone, and so, it seemed, did Alice and Gina, because they both burst out laughing.

"We're having a friendly discussion here, darling," Gina told her husband. "You know that I always try to keep an open mind."

"Anyway," Alice continued, "I was just about to explain that my interest as a scientist is in trying to prove that dolphins *can* have a measurable effect of making people feel better." She paused for a sip of iced tea.

"Alice is studying the effect of sound vibrations on brain waves," Jerry added. "There have already been studies on the effect of sounds we hear, like music, on our emotions, but even sounds we can't hear — ultrasound — can affect us."

"Ultrasound?" Brittany suddenly spoke up from the far end of the table where she'd been talking about tennis with Lauren. "That's something they do in hospitals. My aunt had an ultrasound scan when she was pregnant, to make sure her baby was okay. What does that have to do with dolphins?"

"Ultrasound is the term used for sonic vibrations, or sounds, that we humans can't hear," Alice explained.

"But dolphins can," Jody guessed. She remembered her dad explaining to her, Jimmy, and Sean how important sound was to dolphins; that they find their way around using sound rather than sight.

"Yes," Alice agreed. "Dolphins can hear and make sounds in the ultrasonic range. The sort of ultrasound scan Brittany mentioned can give us information about things we can't see, and dolphins probably use their ultrasound in the same way. Some doctors have suggested

44

ultrasound could be used for healing. It might be used instead of surgery, to destroy a tumor, for example."

Jody was so fascinated she forgot to eat. "Could dolphins do that?" she blurted out.

"Oh, no," Alice said quickly, shaking her head. "I wasn't suggesting that! The ultrasound frequencies used in medicine are much, much higher than anything a dolphin could produce. But there's no doubt that the experience of spending time with dolphins has made many people feel better."

"Feeling loved and accepted makes people feel better about themselves," Jerry added. "People who have pets — or companion animals, as they're sometimes called — are usually healthier and happier than people who live alone."

"And that's not just an animal-lover's opinion," Alice said with a teasing smile at Gina. "There have been scientific studies to prove it!"

"Oops!" exclaimed Jerry with a look at his watch. "I hate to eat and run, but I have to look at some paperwork before the next patient arrives." He got up. "I'll see you all later."

Alice rose and began to clear the table. "I'll get these washed, and then —"

"I'll do it, Mom," Lauren said.

"I'll help you," said Jody.

"That's okay, Jody," said Brittany, starting to help Lauren stack plates. "You run along with your folks and study those dolphins — Lauren and I can manage just fine without you." Her tone was poisonously sweet.

Jody's heart sank.

But Lauren smiled at her. "Up to you," she said, "but I thought we could all go swimming when our food's digested."

"Great," said Jody. It seemed that Brittany hadn't managed to turn Lauren against her, after all. "I love swimming."

"Okay then, clearing up won't take long between the three of us," said Lauren, throwing Jody a dishcloth.

Brittany sulked for a few seconds, then decided to make the best of it. "My mom and I have our own swimming pool at home in West Palm Beach," she bragged.

Lauren laughed. "So do we — and ours has dolphins in it!" She turned away to scrape leftovers off a plate.

"Oh. We're going to swim *with* the dolphins?" Brittany's voice suddenly sounded wary.

"Uh-huh, it'll be the best swim you've ever had," Lauren replied.

But Jody could see from Brittany's face that she wasn't convinced. A few days earlier, Brittany had refused the chance to join the McGraths in the sea to swim with a wild dolphin, and Jody had guessed she was afraid. But whatever Brittany might imagine about wild dolphins, surely she could see that the dolphins at CETA were completely safe!

"I thought the dolphins had to work with your father." Brittany said edgily.

Lauren finished stacking the last of the plates in the dishwasher. "He'll have one in the pool, but the others will be in the sea pen — the lagoon. That's where we're going to swim," she explained.

Jody waited to see if Brittany would come up with some excuse not to swim, but an hour later, Brittany had changed into her swimsuit and accompanied them outside.

Gina had asked Jody to take the twins along and, as usual, they had to be first into the water, giving their war cries as they raced each other. Laughing, Lauren dived in right behind them.

Brittany hesitated on the edge of the water, gazing nervously out at the three dolphins swimming so close to Lauren and the boys. When she saw Jody watching, her expression changed. "What are you staring at?" she demanded angrily.

"Nothing. I just thought . . ." Jody hesitated, feeling awkward.

"You just watch out for your kid brothers, not me," Brittany snapped. With that, she took a deep breath, and dived in.

Shrugging, Jody dived in, too, and swam after the others.

Sean and Jimmy were stroking the dolphins and bombarding Lauren with questions. "What's this one's name? Do they know any tricks? Can we play with them? Will they give us rides?"

"Take it easy," said Lauren, shaking her head against the twins' rapid-fire questions. "Get to know them first — let them get to know you, and then they'll play with you." She pointed to the dolphin Jimmy was stroking. "That one's Rosie. The one behind you is her mother, Maxi. And here comes Nora! Whoops!" She giggled as Nora butted her affectionately.

Jody swam over to join them. She stroked each dolphin in turn, marveling at the wonderfully soft, smooth skin beneath her fingers.

"Sean, don't do that," Lauren said warningly.

"What?" asked Sean in surprise.

Jody turned quickly to see what the twins were up to. Sean was just treading water, but his identical brother had his hand over Rosie's blowhole. "Jimmy, don't!" she said sharply.

"I just want to feel —" His explanation was cut short as Rosie decided she'd had enough and submerged abruptly, slapping her tail to make a small wave that splashed over Jimmy.

He came up sputtering. "Hey! That's not nice!"

"How would you like it if somebody put their hand over your nose and mouth?" Lauren demanded. "You were stopping her from breathing, and *that*'s not nice."

Swimming with Lauren and the twins

"You should know better than that," Jody added.

Jimmy scowled. He looked away from their accusing stares, and noticed Brittany, far away from them, looking miserable at the side of the pool.

"Hey look, the dolphins don't like Brittany!" Jimmy declared.

"Don't be silly, Jimmy," Jody said warningly. A quick glance assured her that Brittany hadn't heard. "Leave her alone," she ordered.

"Yeah, that's what the dolphins are doing," Sean chipped in, deciding to back up his brother. "They're leaving her alone! They won't go near her! Wonder why?"

"Maybe she smells bad," Jimmy said, smirking.

"Jimmy, you watch your mouth!" Jody said sharply. But he had a point, she realized. All three dolphins had approached her and the boys, but none had gone near Brittany.

"Okay, okay, sorry." Jimmy shrugged. "But I'm not making it up — you can see they don't like her."

"It's the other way around," Lauren said quietly.

"Huh?" Jimmy stared at her.

51

Lauren glanced over at Brittany, who straightened up in the water at her look, forced a smile, gave a little wave, and finally began to swim toward her. "All dolphins are good at reading body language, and the CETA dolphins have to be especially good at knowing what people want," Lauren explained. "We couldn't possibly have a dolphin here who might frighten a child. They can tell when people are afraid of them. They won't go near anyone who doesn't want them to."

"You mean Brittany's scared of the dolphins?" Sean didn't speak loudly, but Brittany was too close not to hear him.

Jody saw her flush.

Jimmy couldn't let it alone. "Brittany's a scaredy-cat!"

"I am not," Brittany said angrily.

"Scaredy-cat, scaredy-cat!" Both boys started in.

"Come on, let's get away from these little monsters," Lauren said to Brittany. "I'll race you to the dock."

But Lauren's attempt to distract the other girl failed. Brittany thrust her face close to Jody's. "Did you tell them I was scared?" she demanded.

Jody drew away. "No, of course not," she replied hotly.

"But you think I am, don't you?" Brittany spat, glaring furiously. "Well, I'm not. Just because I'm not crazy about dolphins doesn't mean I'm scared of them. They're tame animals. I know they don't hurt people."

"I know," Jody said, trying to calm her. "The boys are just teasing."

"Nobody thinks you're scared," Lauren said.

"Then why won't the dolphins come to me?" Brittany demanded.

"Um . . ." Lauren bit her lip. "Maybe you're giving off the wrong signals."

"What signals?" Brittany looked baffled.

"Why don't we leave it for another time?" Lauren suggested.

But Brittany persisted. "No!" she said. "I don't happen to think that touching a dolphin is such a big deal, but I'm not letting those kids say I'm scared! Show me how to get a dolphin to come to me," she demanded. Then she must have realized how bossy she sounded, because she added, "Please?" in a desperate little voice as she gazed at Lauren.

Lauren gave in and nodded. "Okay, the main thing is

to be relaxed," she explained. "They're attracted to people who are playful and interested in them. If you try to mimic them in the way you move — pretend you're a dolphin — they'll probably be interested, and come closer. Watch me." Lauren flipped over in the water. She began to wriggle and glide, using her whole body to propel herself through he water.

Jody grinned as she watched, remembering her own clumsy attempts to mimic the graceful, powerful movements of a dolphin.

Lauren's demonstration was cut short by Rosie, who rolled through the water to rub herself against the girl. The two of them swam together in harmony for a few moments as Jody and Brittany watched.

"Wow," Brittany murmured.

Surprised, Jody realized that even Brittany was impressed by the beauty of the sight, and the obvious affection between Lauren and Rosie.

Then, wrapping her arms around the dolphin, Lauren surfaced. She gave a low whistle, and rubbed her face against the side of Rosie's head. She seemed to be whispering something. Jody wondered if Lauren was

54

telling Rosie to make friends with Brittany. Then a small sound made her look around.

Another dolphin, Maxi, had approached Brittany. She was only inches away, lying sideways, watching the girl with one eye.

Jody held her breath as she waited to see what would happen next.

Brittany was very still. But she didn't look frightened.

The dolphin began to move. She swam in a slow, close circle around Brittany, then dived lower in the water, pointing her beak at the girl's body and making a stream of distinct clicking sounds. After a while, Maxi surfaced and rolled onto her back, showing her belly.

For a moment, Brittany didn't move.

Jody bit her lip, willing her to respond.

Finally, slowly, cautiously, Brittany stretched out one arm. Her hand came to rest on the dolphin's underside. She began to stroke Maxi, gently at first, and then more firmly. A look of wonder spread over her face, and she began to smile. "You like that, do you?" she murmured. She seemed to have forgotten everyone else, as if she and Maxi were alone together. And, for once, she looked relaxed, almost happy.

June 26 — bedtime.
Brittany was a lot easier to be around this evening. For once, she didn't jump on everything I said, or make me feel left out by hogging Lauren's attention the whole time. Could this be due to what happened with Maxi? Who would have thought a dolphin could cure bad temper!

Kim came over and watched us while we were swimming, and later I heard her talking to Mom. She thought Brittany must be an orphan or something. She said Brittany was such a "sad girl," and that she had noticed Maxi "mothering" her. She said watching them together made her think of someone else Maxi had helped: a little girl whose father had died in a car crash.

I wonder . . . maybe Brittany does feel her mother has abandoned her . . . and Maxi is helping. . . .

4

The next morning Alice announced that she had borrowed four bicycles so that Lauren could take their
visitors on a tour of Cedar Key. "And I've packed you a
picnic, so you won't have to hurry back for lunch," she
added, smiling.

Sean and Jimmy were thrilled. Living on a boat, they
had missed their bikes. Now, they couldn't even wait
to finish breakfast before rushing out to inspect the
borrowed wheels.

Jody felt torn. She was fascinated by the work being
done at CETA and wanted to see more of it. But it

would be fun to explore the island, too. She looked over at the others. Her heart sank as she saw the now familiar stormy expression on Brittany's face. Her good mood hadn't lasted very long!

"It'll be too hot to go out on bikes," Brittany groaned. She looked from Lauren to Gina for agreement.

"Not if you go out right now," Gina said. "This is the coolest part of the day."

Brittany stared down at the toast on her plate. "I'd rather go swimming," she said stubbornly.

"Take your suits," Alice suggested. "Lauren, you could take them to Sea Horse Bay."

"Sea Horse Bay?" Jody repeated, her attention caught by the name.

"It's a really cool place," Lauren told her. "You can see pygmy sea horses floating in the shallows. They're wonderful! And we can swim off the edge of the sand-bank, where it's a little deeper."

"Just be careful of the current," Alice warned. "Because the water isn't deep, people tend to think it's safe, but the current is very strong, so you do have to pay attention."

"I know all that, Mom," Lauren said, in a put-upon tone.

"Well, our guests don't," her mother pointed out. "Make sure Sean and Jimmy understand. Enjoy yourselves!"

Brittany looked sulky, but she didn't say anything. Jody thought she must have realized that if she complained she'd get left behind on her own.

"Do you know anything about the Florida Keys?" Lauren asked as they got ready to set off, rubbing themselves with sunscreen and mosquito repellent.

"I know! Key is another word for island," Sean offered.

Lauren nodded. "They are islands, but most of them, including this one, are joined together by a hundred-mile stretch of highway — Highway 1. But we're not going on the highway. We can get around Cedar Key on local roads and trails. That'll be more fun, and it'll give us a chance to see more wildlife."

"Oh, boy, I hope we see some alligators," Jimmy said excitedly.

Jody shuddered. "I hope we don't."

Brittany smiled unpleasantly. "Don't tell me Jody is scared of something?"

Jody could feel her face going red. "I'm not scared — I just don't like them much," she insisted. "Or rattlesnakes, or water moccasins."

"I'm not crazy about them, either," Lauren said. She finished fastening the bag containing their picnic onto her bicycle and wheeled it into position on the driveway. "Come on, let's head for Sea Horse Bay!"

Jody's heart lifted as they pedaled away. It was sunny and warm, already shaping up to be another blazingly hot day, but Jody had spent her whole life in Florida, and was too used to the climate to mind the heat. Patches of trees — Lauren had said that they were known here as "hammocks" — provided intervals of shade as they traveled, rolling along the quiet trails that crisscrossed the little island.

"When are we going to stop?" Brittany asked after a while. "I'm dying of thirst!"

Jody was starting to feel tired and thirsty, too, but she didn't want to complain, especially since her little brothers were still going strong.

"Lauren glanced back over her shoulder. "Nearly there!" she promised. "It'll be worth it!"

A few minutes later Lauren came to a halt, jumping off her bike in the shade of a mangrove hammock. She pointed to where the trees ended. A clean, empty, sandy beach gleamed in the sun. "Sea Horse Bay," she said, sounding a little breathless.

Jody forgot her thirst and gazed out at the blue, shallow water of the sandbank. She smiled. "It's beautiful." And then her eyes went beyond, to the deeper water. She couldn't help searching for signs of dolphins wherever she went. But she saw none here.

"Water, water," gasped Jimmy. He dropped to his hands and knees and began to drag himself across the ground. Seconds later, Sean was rolling on the sand, clutching his throat.

Lauren handed Brittany and Jody soft drinks out of her saddlebag, then took one for herself. She ignored Sean and Jimmy until they jumped up, indignant.

"Hey, what about us? Don't we get drinks?" Jimmy demanded.

The calm before the storm . . .

"Sure, all you have to do is ask." Smiling sweetly, Lauren took two more cans out for them.

For the next minute the silence was broken only by thirsty gulping sounds.

Jody finished her drink and stowed the empty can away in her knapsack. She breathed in deeply, enjoying the salty tang of the air and the peaceful surroundings, and then she noticed that they were not the only people on the beach. At the other end of the bay, a dark-haired woman in a long white dress was walking along with a little boy who looked about five years old.

Suddenly, the boy veered away from the woman and splashed into the water. The woman called to him, but Jody couldn't hear her words. The boy didn't look around or respond in any way to her call. He just kept walking through the water.

The woman stopped and hiked up her long, gauzy dress. Balancing on one leg, she tugged off one sandal and called again. This time, her voice carried across the beach. "Wait, Hal! Stop right there!"

The boy must have heard her, too, but he didn't stop.

He didn't even pause. He kept on walking through the water. But the water was only up to his ankles.

The woman must have realized he was in no danger, too. She looked at the sandal in her hand, not bothering to take off the other one and run after him. "Hal! Come back here!" she called. But she no longer sounded urgent, and didn't seem to expect a response.

"That's a very bad little boy," said Brittany, sounding amused.

Jody kept watching. Something was making her uneasy. There was something wrong, but she couldn't put her finger on it . . . until she realized it was the darkening shade of blue in the water where the little boy was headed. Maybe, with her dark glasses on, the woman couldn't see where the line of darker blue water marked the point where the sandbank ended, Jody thought.

Urgently, she turned to Lauren. "It looks to me as if the sandbank ends just there," she said, pointing. "That little boy is walking toward much deeper water!"

Lauren gasped. "You're right, Jody," she said. "We have to stop him, before he goes too far!"

There was no time to think about it. Jody grabbed her bike and pushed off, pedaling as hard as she could.

Too late! The little boy reached the end of the sandbank. His arms flew up as he slipped, dropping out of sight beneath the water.

The woman on the beach screamed and started to run, but then she stumbled on her single sandal, falling to the ground.

Jody went flying past the woman, straight into the shallow water. Then she leapcd off the bike, letting it fall, and plunged into the deeper water.

She looked around wildly for some sign of the little boy and saw his bright blue T-shirt. He was facedown in the water. Her stomach lurched with fear, but she grabbed the cloth of the shirt and pulled the boy to her.

As she lifted him out of the water she was relieved to hear him give a deep, choking cough. "Are you okay?" she demanded.

The boy's eyes were shut tight against the salt water. He sputtered and spat, and then wriggled in her grasp. His feet were on the seabed now, but the waves lapped at his chin. Jody was afraid to let him go, fearful that he would slip under again, or that the current might pull him away.

"Hang on to me," she told him. "We're just going back onto the sandbank — then I'll let you go."

He didn't resist her efforts to pull him into the shallower water, but he didn't help, either. Jody remembered how he had seemed to ignore the woman's calls, and wondered if he was deaf.

"Is my son all right?" cried the woman as she took hold of the boy, hauling him onto dry land. Her voice wobbled as she said, "Thank goodness you were there — how can I ever thank you?"

"I think he's okay," Jody told her. "Just a little —" She stopped. She was going to say "frightened" but as she looked at the boy, she realized that was wrong. Apart from being soaking wet, he looked unaffected by his near-drowning experience, even struggling against his mother's attempt to hug him. He pulled against her, gazing out to sea.

Jody went to fetch her abandoned bicycle, hoping the salt water hadn't damaged the gears. By the time she got it back to the beach, she found Lauren, Brittany, Sean, and Jimmy clustered around the woman and the little boy, offering them towels, food, and drink. Sean even pulled off his own T-shirt and offered it to the boy.

The woman accepted a towel to dry her son. While she rubbed him he stood like a statue, his face blank and expressionless.

"What's your name?" the woman asked Jody. "Where do you live?"

Jody introduced herself and the others. "Lauren lives here on Cedar Key with her parents. We're just visiting," she explained.

The woman nodded and smiled at each of them in turn. "I'm Janet Davis. This is my son, Hal. We're visiting, too. . . . We came up from Key West for the day. It seemed so safe and quiet. Hal has a thing about the sea, he really loves it. I didn't want him to go in the water, but I could see how shallow it was . . . or I thought I could. . . . I thought he was safe." She bit her lip and gently stroked her son's wet brown hair.

"You should teach him how to swim, then he would

be safer," Jody said. She felt a little awkward, giving advice to an adult, but it seemed so obvious.

"Yes, of course, but it's very difficult. . . ." Janet Davis's voice trailed off.

Hal pulled away, heading for the water again. His mother held him firmly. "No, Hal. Not now. Stay with me."

Lauren was staring intently at the boy. Then she raised her calm eyes and asked his mother, "Is Hal autistic?"

Janet Davis raised her eyebrows in surprise. "Why, yes, he is. But how did you know?"

"My father is a psychologist," Lauren explained. "Autism is one of his special interests. I've seen a lot of the children he's helped."

"Really!" Not taking her eyes from Lauren's face, Janet caught her son firmly as he tried to move away again. "What's your father's name?"

"Dr. Jerry Rozakis," Lauren replied.

"Maybe I should talk to him," the woman said eagerly. "We've seen other specialists, of course — all over the world."

"You should talk to my dad," Lauren agreed. She

went on proudly, "He's had wonderful results helping autistic children with dolphin-assisted therapy."

Suddenly, something seemed to shut down in the woman's face. She had been so interested, but now she looked wary.

"It's really good," Jody jumped in, eager to recapture Janet Davis's interest. "I've seen the way the kids respond to the dolphins — it really makes a big difference. The center is called CETA — that stands for Cctaceans as Educational and Therapeutic Associates. Lauren's dad says the dolphins are the teachers, and it's really true!"

But it was no good. Jody had the feeling that no matter what she said, it wouldn't register. Janet Davis had withdrawn from the conversation. For some reason, she just didn't like the idea of dolphin-assisted therapy. The warmth had gone.

The woman's expression was remote, almost chilly, as she handed Lauren back her towel. "Thank you very much for everything. I am very grateful for your help."

Jimmy had been trying to catch the little boy's attention by making silly faces, without success.

Now Sean leaned in close. "Hey, want to come look at our bikes? I'll give you a ride."

The little boy stared blankly out to sea. His mother pulled him closer to her and began to move away. "I think we'd better leave now."

"Please, let Jerry Rozakis explain what he does," Jody insisted. "While you're here, you really ought to come and visit CETA, and see for yourself. It might help." She was starting to feel a little desperate.

But it was no good.

"I'll think about what you've said," Janet Davis said, her voice now icy. "Come, Hal. We're going."

Janet Davis and her son walked away along the beach without looking back.

5

June 27 — bedtime.

One of the things that is so great about CETA is that the dolphins really are free. Dolphins in captivity aren't as healthy as wild dolphins, and they don't live as long. Even when they are kept in large pens and have lots of company, they suffer more from stress and diseases.

Alice and Jerry do their best to keep the CETA dolphins healthy and happy. Once a week they open the sea gate, and the dolphins can go out into the open sea if they want.

Alice talked about a scientist called John Lilly, who

came up with the idea that people and dolphins could work together as equals. Instead of thinking they "own" dolphins, keeping them like slaves for their entire lives, buying and selling them, people who work with dolphins should treat them fairly and let them go after they've finished their "term of service."

I can't wait to see what happens tomorrow. It's Sunday, and the sea gate will be opened. I wonder if the CETA dolphins will go out and play with Apollo and his gang?!

It was Sunday morning and Jody had been too excited to eat much breakfast. "Can we go out and watch the dolphins as the sea gates are opened?" she asked, the minute she'd shoveled down some cornflakes in record time.

"I'm afraid they'll go too far out in the lagoon for you to see very much," Alice began. "Unless . . ." She broke off uncertainly.

"Oh, Mom, can we go out in *Princess?*" Lauren asked eagerly.

Alice looked at Jody's parents. "Jerry and I have too much paperwork to get through today, but . . . would either of you feel comfortable handling a small speed-boat?"

Craig's eyebrows lifted, his eyes gleamed, and he rubbed his hands together briskly. "Lead me to it!"

"I think you can trust him with your boat," Gina said, laughing. "At least, with Lauren and Jody along to keep him under control."

"You're not going?" Alice asked Gina.

Gina shook her head. "Maddie and I need to edit some of the video footage we shot during the week."

"Not much of a day of rest," Craig commented.

"It never is around here, except for the dolphins," Alice said as she walked over to the storeroom. The dolphins' food supply was kept there, and it also housed a control panel for all the outside lights and the underwater gates.

"Dad never gets any time off," Lauren told Jody. "Even when there aren't any patients, there's always some work that has to be done."

The dolphins seemed to know what day it was, because they were waiting by the sea gates. Jody saw a little ripple go through the water as there was a motorized hum and then, with a clanking sound, the underwater gates swung open.

Rosie shot through first, followed closely by her mother. Jody thought she caught a glimpse of Nick and Nora deep beneath the water, but she couldn't be sure. She raised her eyes to stare out at the calm waters of the lagoon, searching for some sign of the wild dolphins, but nothing showed above the surface.

"We'll see them better from *Princess.*" Lauren spoke as if she'd read Jody's mind. "I'm so glad your dad is going to take us! I'll go get Brittany!"

Jody's heart sank. She turned to her father. "Should I go get the twins?"

"You can tell them what we're doing, but I doubt you'll tempt them away from those bicycles," Craig said with a grin.

As Craig had predicted, Sean and Jimmy weren't interested. Their plans for the day involved bicycles, exploring, and snake hunting. The boys had been strictly forbidden to try to catch or touch any snakes, but Sean kept a careful, constantly updated list of every snake he spotted.

On her way back, Jody met Lauren by herself. "Brittany wanted to do something on the computer," she said with a shrug.

Jody nodded, trying not to show how relieved she was. She couldn't tell if Lauren was disappointed, but for herself she was glad to have a break from Brittany's moods, and the chance to spend time with Lauren on her own.

Princess was a small, rather elderly powerboat that was berthed in the lagoon on the other side of the sea pen. Lauren led the way along a narrow, winding path at the back of the house. They jumped in and Craig swiftly got the boat moving, heading out to sea.

"There they are!" Lauren was the first to spot the group of dolphins.

Craig powered down, and then, as they drew close to the dolphins, cut the engine. They floated in silence. Jody leaned over the side, trying to count the constantly moving group of sleek, shining gray animals. Three . . . four . . . six . . . eight?

"There's Rosie," Lauren cried. "See the scar above her eye? Who's that with her? Is it one of the wild dolphins?"

As Lauren spoke, Rosie and the other dolphin leaped high into the air, passing so close to the side of the boat that Jody felt the spray on her face. She blinked and looked again. Was that a faint, harp-shaped marking on his jaw? She decided that it was. "I think that's Apollo!" she cried, thrilled.

It seemed the dolphins were excited, too. Jody had never seen them leap so high, or so often. They were chasing one another through water and air, bumping their bodies together, leaping over and under each other in some complicated pattern.

"It's almost like they're dancing," Lauren said. "Oh, look, there's Nick! But that's not Nora he's with . . . that's another one of the wild dolphins."

Jody shielded her eyes from the sun. "I think that's Poseidon. He's the biggest of this group. That little one over there is Triton. There's Hermes! And I think that one is Artemis, although it could be Castor or Pollux."

"Oh, they all have names from Greek mythology," Lauren noted. "Cool! Whose idea was that?"

Jody felt herself blushing. "Mine, I guess. I named

Apollo first, so when we met the rest of his group, it seemed like a good idea."

They spent nearly an hour watching from *Princess* as the dolphins played. Jody longed to get into the water and swim with them, but her father vetoed that suggestion. All too soon, it seemed to her, he said it was time to go back.

Craig gazed out at the dolphins, who were now swimming farther away from the boat, and from the lagoon itself. They seemed to be headed for the open sea. He frowned. "I'd suggest following them, but we might run out of fuel. I hope CETA isn't about to lose its entire nonhuman staff," he added uneasily.

"Oh, they'll come back for their next meal," Lauren said confidently. "They always do."

Maxi had returned by midday, and Lauren and Jody helped Alice to feed her.

"Won't the others be hungry?" Jody felt worried. She knew that dolphins needed to eat a lot.

Alice raised her eyes to stare out at the lagoon. There was a line between her eyes, but she made an effort to smile at the girls. "They don't have to be. As the saying goes, there's plenty more fish in the sea!"

"Probably they'll feed with the wild dolphins," Jody guessed. Then she frowned. "But why did Maxi come back?"

"Maxi has spent nearly her whole life in captivity, a lot longer than the others," Alice explained. "You could say she's lost her hunting instincts. She relies on us to be fed." She tossed another fish to the waiting dolphin as she spoke.

Jody thought about it. "Then how about her daughter? If Rosie's never been a wild dolphin, how does she know how to hunt?"

"We taught her . . . with the help of Nick and Nora," Alice replied. "We were determined she should be able to fend for herself because someday she may want to go and live free." Alice gestured around at the lagoon. "The dolphins here can keep their hunting instincts because they're still living in the sea, not in a small manmade pool where the concrete walls would bounce sounds right back at them. You know that dolphins use sound to hunt and to get around?" She looked at Jody.

Jody nodded. "It's called echolocation, isn't it?" she said. "Dolphins can find their way around in the ocean, and track down their food by using sound." She tossed Maxi the last of the fish.

"That's right," Alice replied. "Maxi wasn't so fortunate. Before she came to us, she was kept in a big, concrete tank. If she'd tried to use echolocation to find food the way she would in the open sea, the sounds would have bounced off the walls — it wouldn't have worked. She might even have found it painful. So she would have stopped doing it. And you know that if you stop practicing a skill, you lose it. That's what seems to happen with dolphins, and that's why just releasing all captive dolphins into the wild, as some people would like to do, isn't so smart." Alice turned the bucket upside down to show Maxi it was empty. "That's all you get, honey."

Maxi chattered at them, and opened her mouth to show her teeth before sinking below the surface and swimming slowly away.

*   *   *

By five o'clock there was still no sign of the other dolphins. As everyone gathered in the kitchen, Alice Rozakis couldn't hide her concern.

"They've never stayed out so long," Lauren confided to Jody and Brittany. She tugged at her braid in a worried way.

"Have you got some way of calling them?" Gina asked.

Jerry nodded. "Time to ring the dinner bell," he said. "If that doesn't get them . . . well, then all we can do is wait and hope they'll decide to come back."

They all went outside. Jody hadn't noticed the bell before, and now she wondered how she'd missed it. It was a big, old-fashioned brass bell suspended from a wooden archway, with a rope hanging down.

"It's an old-fashioned school bell," Alice explained. "It was a present from a friend. It's more than a hundred and fifty years old." She grasped hold of the rope and pulled. The loud, clanging sound of the bell tolled out.

"Calling all tardy young scholars — and dolphins," said Craig, shading his eyes against the sun.

Jody peered out at the glittering water of the lagoon and held her breath, wishing for a response.

Alice continued to toll the bell, and they all waited in silence, watching and hoping.

Lauren was the first to see them. "Look, it's a whole group!"

Now Jody also spotted the dark, curving fins poking through the waves. She counted ten. "It must be Apollo and his group *and* your dolphins," she said. "Maybe they've come to say good-bye?"

To everyone's astonishment, all ten dolphins came through the sea gate, into the sea pen, and swam in close to the shore.

"There's Nick and Nora, and Rosie!" Lauren cried out their names with delight.

Jody recognized the wild dolphins as well.

"But why have they all come?" Lauren asked.

"Yours must have told them what a great place CETA is," Craig joked. "They decided they like people, after meeting us, and now they want to know more about us."

"Maybe they've come for the food," Maddie suggested. "They've never heard of anything like it — all the fish you can eat, without the bother of having to catch them yourself!"

Jerry groaned and ran his hand through his curly hair. "They'd eat us out of house and home! We don't have enough fish to feed ten hungry dolphins!"

"I don't think we should even try to feed them." Alice had left the bell and was standing beside her husband, her hand resting on his arm. "Probably they came along out of curiosity, and they'll soon leave. I'm sure ours will wait to be fed."

Sure enough, most of the wild dolphins soon decided they had seen enough of the fenced-in lagoon, and swam away out to sea. Only Apollo remained behind with the four CETA dolphins.

"That's the dolphin we've told you about, Jody's special friend," Craig said. "It was probably his idea to come here in the first place."

"Well, I don't mind giving him a few fish, as a thank-you for bringing our dolphins safely home," Jerry said. He was looking much happier now.

Apollo poked his head out of the water and reared up right in front of Jody.

Rosie and Apollo are off!

She whistled at him, trying as best she could to imitate the sound she remembered, and was thrilled when he whistled back.

Rosie rose out of the water right beside Apollo. She whistled, too.

Then both Rosie and Apollo sank beneath the water and swam away. They were headed for the sea gate.

"Rosie, no!" called Lauren, sounding worried.

"Rosie!" Alice ran for the bell and began to pull the

rope. As it clanged loudly in the air, Nick and Nora became excited, jostling each other at the side of the pen and making impatient clicking sounds. Maxi joined them. It was obvious they knew what the bell meant, and were eager to be fed.

But Rosie did not respond. She and Apollo were heading for the freedom of the open sea just as fast as they could go.

6

June 28 — bedtime.

Rosie is still gone.

Lauren's parents went out in Princess to try to find her. She came right up to the boat once, but nothing they tried would make her follow them back to the center. After a while she swam off with Apollo and they had to give up.

They decided to leave the sea gate open tonight, just in case Rosie comes back. Jerry was really gloomy. He said maybe it would be better if the other three dolphins decided to swim away tonight and join Apollo's group. Then they'd have to close down CETA and find some less stressful work. I hope he didn't really mean it.

Lauren is really unhappy — she misses Rosie so much — but she is being brave. She said all that really matters is that Rosie is okay, wherever she is.

I can't help feeling guilty. WE brought Apollo here, and if it hadn't been for that, Rosie would never have gone away.

In the morning, there was still no sign of Rosie. Jody rushed outside with Lauren first thing, leaving Brittany still yawning in her bed. They were greeted by creaking calls from Nick and Nora, eager for their breakfast.

Tight-lipped, Jerry went to shut the sea gate. "Bud should be here by now," he muttered.

"I'll feed them, Dad," Lauren volunteered.

"Thanks, sweetheart." Jerry patted his daughter on the shoulder before vanishing into the house.

"I'll help," Jody said, and followed Lauren to the storage room to fill buckets with the last of the fish.

Lauren told her there would be a fresh delivery later in the day, and slipped the thick cord with a whistle on it over her head.

Brittany appeared just as they were lugging the buckets down to the waterside. "Did your dolphin come back?" she asked Lauren.

Wordless, Lauren shook her head. She began to fling fish into the eager, waiting jaws of Nick and Nora. Jody followed her example.

"Hey, Maxi, it's breakfast time," Lauren called.

Jody looked around but could see no sign of the third dolphin. Her heart gave a painful lurch. "Did Maxi leave, too?"

"No, she's over there." Lauren nodded toward the other side of the sea pen. "I don't know what's wrong with her; she's acting like she's not interested."

Now Jody made out the shape of the mother dolphin, swimming listlessly up and down, with her blowhole just above the surface.

"She's missing her daughter," said Brittany, staring intently into the water.

Jody turned to look at her in surprise. Could this be the girl who thought dolphins were boring, dumb animals?

Lauren nodded, tossing more fish to Nick and Nora.

"You're right," she agreed. "Maxi and Rosie have never been apart. And Rosie is still pretty young. In the wild, she'd probably stay with her mother for a couple more years." She frowned unhappily, then turned to Brittany. "It's not going to do her any good not to eat. Do you want to try and tempt her?"

"Me?" Brittany's eyes widened. She hesitated and then slowly nodded. "Okay. I'll try." With a grimace, she picked a fish out of the bucket and crouched down, holding it by the tail over the water.

Nick swam up and grabbed the fish, taking Brittany by surprise. She shrieked and fell back on her heels.

Jody gave a snort of laughter.

Brittany glared at her. "Real funny, Jody! I'm trying to do something nice, here. The least you could do is keep those two greedy-guts out of the way!"

"I'm sorry," Jody said meekly, struggling to keep a straight face.

Lauren pointed to the other side of the pool. "We'll take these two over there. Brittany, why don't you take that bucket down to the dock, and try to feed Maxi from there?"

As Brittany nodded, Lauren blew a short blast on the whistle to get Nick and Nora's attention. They responded quickly, and followed the two girls around to the other side.

"Don't feed them too fast," Lauren advised Jody. "We can drag it out and give Brittany a better chance to coax Maxi."

Jody looked across to the dock. Brittany was now sitting on the edge with her bare feet dangling into the water, and she was saying something in a low, gentle tone. After a few moments, Maxi responded by coming to investigate. She nudged Brittany's feet. With a giggle, the girl pulled her feet out of the water, and Maxi poked her beak out after them.

Quick as a flash, Brittany swung a fish at the dolphin. Her mouth opened for it, and, once she'd had a taste, Maxi regained her appetite enough to gulp down several more. But she didn't eat as much as normal, and once she'd decided she'd had enough, neither Brittany nor Lauren could coax her back for more.

"Never mind," said Alice when they told her about it later. "You did well."

Brittany gives Maxi her lunch

Returning to the house, the girls had washed their hands, and were ready for their own breakfast. The boys had already gone off to play, and Jerry to work, but Alice, Gina, Craig, and Maddie were still sipping cups of coffee at the big round table.

"It's not surprising if Maxi is grieving . . . her appetite will be less than usual, but as long as she doesn't starve herself, she'll be okay," Lauren's mother went on as the girls poured themselves bowls of cereal.

"But will you?" Jody's mother, sipping a cup of coffee, leaned forward to look closely at her friend. "Can you manage with one less dolphin?"

Alice managed a pained smile. "We'll have to, won't we? It'll mean more work for the other dolphins — and Rosie was shaping up to be one of the very best — but, well . . ." She shrugged and stared down into her coffee. "Actually, we've been offered another dolphin from a Sea-Life Center that doesn't really have the space to keep him. We weren't sure that we could afford the price they're asking, and Jerry already has about as much as he can do without having to start training a newcomer, but with Rosie gone, I don't think we have any choice."

"I have an idea," Brittany said suddenly.

They all turned to look at her. She reddened at the attention, but explained her idea. "I could ask my dad to take us out on *Dolphin Dreamer* to look for Rosie. If we found her, maybe we could tempt her with some fish, like I did with Maxi, and she might follow us back to the lagoon. I'm sure once she got close enough to hear her mother she'd want to come back to her." As she finished speaking, Brittany dropped her eyes and stared down at the table.

Jody was too astonished to speak. It was an idea she wished she'd had first. And for Brittany to think about something other than her own problems was amazing!

"That's a great idea, Brittany," Lauren said enthusiastically. She pushed her empty cereal bowl away from her and looked at her mother. "Can we try it?"

They all looked at Gina, who said slowly, "Well, I don't see why not. Knowing Harry, he's probably getting bored with Key West by now and would be happy for a chance to spend the day sailing."

"You could take my car," Alice said to Gina.

Gina smiled warmly at her old friend, then looked at the three girls who were waiting, breathless, for her to speak. "Okay," she said decisively. "Let's do it!"

Maddie and Craig decided they wanted to go along, which meant the twins had to be included, so in the end the expedition proved to be an unexpected reunion of the whole crew — with the exception of Dr. Jefferson Taylor.

The sight of *Dolphin Dreamer* brought a smile to Jody's face. As her feet touched the deck for the first time in four days, she felt she had come home again. She filled her lungs with sea air and lifted her face to the blazing sun.

As they sailed out of the marina at Key West, the sound of nautical phrases barked out in Harry's English accent or Cam's drawling Southern tones was like music to her ears. Jody had been too interested in all that was going on at CETA to really miss life on board *Dolphin Dreamer*, but now she realized how great it was to be back.

Looking at Harry's weather-beaten, bearded face, and Cam's rugged good looks, she mentally added: and to have the whole family together again. Even though they weren't actually related, she had come to feel that the *Dolphin Dreamer* crew was part of her family.

In a minute, Jody decided, she would go below to chat with Mei Lin and find out what she'd been up to in Key West. But right now, with the wind ruffling her hair and the sun warm on her bare arms and face, all she wanted to do was lean against the rail and enjoy the wonderful sensation of being where she belonged, at sea again, in the company of her family and friends.

Despite such a promising start, the expedition was not a success. They spotted a group of dolphins once, but they were too far away to be identified. Jody found herself wishing, for once, that Dr. Taylor were on board. He had tagged Hermes, one of the members of Apollo's group, and could have used his equipment to tell them where he was. Chances were that wherever Hermes was to be found, Apollo and Rosie would not be far away.

But the dolphins in the distance did not seem interested in approaching *Dolphin Dreamer*. Harry and Cam enjoyed the challenge of trying to catch up with them, but it proved impossible. The speedy creatures soon disappeared, not to be seen again.

Late in the afternoon they sailed into the lagoon where CETA was located. Standing beside Lauren, Jody strained her eyes for any sign of dolphin activity on this side of the fence.

"Well, it was a good idea," Craig said quietly, resting

his hand on Jody's shoulder. "But I think we might as well accept that it didn't work."

"It was a terrible idea," Brittany snapped from her place on Lauren's other side. "If I'd realized this boat was too slow to catch up to a bunch of dolphins, I would never have suggested it! What a boring, wasted day!"

Jody saw Lauren bite her lip as she looked at Brittany. Then she said in a low voice, "It was a *good* idea. You were trying to help, and I'm glad we got the chance to look for Rosie, thanks to you and your dad. You couldn't have done any more."

Brittany's scowl disappeared as she saw that Lauren meant it. "I really wanted us to find her and bring her back," she said quietly. "So Maxi would cheer up." Then she made a face. "Anyway, I can't wait to get off this boat again. Of all the boring ways to spend time, sailing has got to be the absolute worst!"

Jody winced, hoping that Harry hadn't heard.

Lauren turned to Craig. "Could we get off here instead of sailing all the way back to Key West?" She gazed up at him appealingly.

"You want us to dump you in the lagoon?" Craig pretended to be shocked.

"I'm not getting my clothes wet," Brittany said with a scowl.

Lauren turned to the other girl to explain. "If we sail around past the sea pen to the bay where *Princess* is berthed, we can get off at the dock and walk up to the house."

Craig nodded. "Okay. I'll go and tell Harry."

There was a black limousine with a driver waiting outside the CETA office when Jody, Lauren, and Brittany arrived back.

Jody looked at Lauren in surprise. "Is that for one of the patients?"

Wide-eyed, Lauren shook her head. "Not unless it's a new one!"

They went through the archway into the central courtyard and found Lauren's father talking to a smartly dressed man.

Brittany gave a little gasp, and Jody looked at her in

surprise. Before she could ask her if she knew the man, Jerry had caught sight of them.

"Ah, here's Jody now!" he called out. "She's the one you want to talk to."

"Me!" Jody exclaimed in surprise.

"This is Gavin Davis," Jerry said.

"I'm Hal's father," the man explained, reaching out and grasping Jody's hand tightly. "I'm sorry it's taken me so long to come over here to thank you personally for saving my son."

Jody felt herself blush. "Oh, well, I'm glad I was there. I'm glad I could help."

"So are we," Gavin Davis replied. "More than I can possibly say." He paused, still holding her hand, gray eyes shining with emotion behind gold-rimmed glasses.

Jerry stepped in to introduce him to everyone else. Jody noticed that Brittany seemed completely awe-struck, and couldn't stop staring at Gavin Davis. She wondered why. Although he seemed very friendly and likeable, surely he was a little too old to inspire a crush!

Gavin Davis cleared his throat. "I was just about to

tell Dr. Rozakis, I've been very impressed by what he's shown me today. As you know, my son Hal is autistic. A couple of years ago, my wife and I wondered if swimming with dolphins might help him. We wrote to CETA and one other place in Florida, but both had waiting lists. Then we heard about a place in Mexico where anyone could swim with dolphins, at anytime. We were too impatient to wait, so we decided to try that." He shook his head, his expression turning grave.

"Well, we were horrified by the conditions we found there. The dolphins were kept in tiny little pools, separated from one another, and they were never allowed to rest. Each one was forced to share the pool with dozens of visitors every day. We even saw people teasing and tormenting the poor animals, who couldn't escape." He continued his story in a low, sad voice.

Jody felt sick at the thought.

"No wonder your wife didn't seem so keen when I told her about CETA," Lauren said.

Gavin Davis nodded. "What we saw was so awful, it made us give up the idea of visiting anywhere else that kept captive dolphins. But we did like the idea of introducing him to wild dolphins, so I bought a yacht. We spend most of our vacation time on it," he concluded.

"But Hal can't swim," Jody pointed out. Surely Gavin hadn't forgotten that!

Gavin looked rueful. "Yes, that is a problem. We've tried and tried to teach him, but we just can't get him to concentrate!"

"The dolphins here could teach him," Lauren blurted out, a wide smile on her usually serious face.

"I really do hope so," said Gavin Davis. Turning back to Jerry, he said, "I'm sure you still have a waiting list, but I'm hoping that you'll make an exception, and squeeze us in for a few sessions, as soon as possible. We're staying here in Florida for the next two weeks."

Jody turned eagerly to look at Jerry Rozakis. She felt sure he couldn't refuse.

But the short, bearded psychologist shook his graying head. "I'm sorry, Mr. Davis," he said gruffly. "But it's just not possible."

"Oh, Daddy!" Lauren cried. Jody felt as distressed as her friend sounded.

"I'll happily pay twice your going rate," Gavin Davis said, "Or more. Add a bonus for every session — name your price!"

But Jerry would not back down. "This isn't about money," he explained. "With Rosie missing, the other three dolphins will have heavier schedules than usual. It wouldn't be fair to any of the other patients to cancel their sessions —"

"Oh, no, I'm not asking you to do that," the man insisted. "But maybe, in your spare time, in the evenings, or next weekend," he suggested hopefully.

"Spare time!" Jerry gave an angry, barking laugh. "What's that? I already work practically every hour there is . . . if I'm not with the patients there's paperwork, routine maintenance, making sure everything gets done. Maybe you're going to suggest I should give up eating, or sleeping?"

There was an awkward silence.

"I'm sorry," Jerry began, with a sigh. "It's not your fault. . . ."

"No, no," said Gavin Davis calmly. He sounded thoughtful. "I simply hadn't realized that you ran everything yourself. You could save yourself a lot of stress if you learned to delegate."

"Oh, right!" Jerry exploded. "Who am I supposed to delegate *to*? Kim's a great help, but she's still a trainee, and she's probably going to leave next year and go back for her Ph.D. Bud does most of the maintenance work, but it's really too big a job for just one man. Alice does what she can, but she has her own work. . . ."

"Have you thought about hiring more staff?" Gavin Davis asked in a businesslike way.

Jerry gave a bitter laugh. "Thought about it! Dreamed about it, more like. I just can't afford it."

"You might find that with reorganization the additional staff would pay for themselves," Mr. Davis said. Pushing his glasses up on his nose, he leaned forward to look into Jerry's eyes. "Will you let me do something for you?" he asked. "Consider it my inadequate thanks for Jody's quick thinking. Make time this week — two hours — for a meeting with me and my financial advisor. You won't regret it, you have my word that it will be two hours well spent. You'll answer our questions, and we'll make some suggestions. You don't have to follow them, of course. Just let us try to help. Will you do it?"

For a moment, Jody was sure Jerry was going to refuse. She held her breath, waiting.

Then Jerry shrugged. "Okay. Two hours. But it'll have to be in the evening." He looked a little bemused, as if surprised by his own agreement.

Gavin Davis nodded. "Should we say Wednesday? Eight o'clock?" When this was accepted, he turned to Jody again. "I'd also like to do a little something special for you. Would you enjoy a day out on my yacht?"

Before she could answer, Jody was surprised to hear Brittany's voice, breathless with excitement, saying, "Oh, yes, that would be wonderful! We'd *love* to come!"

The man smiled. "That's great." He winked at Jody. "Feel free to bring along any other friends or family members who'd like to come — there'll be plenty of food for lunch. We'll make it a party! I'll send the motorboat to pick you up tomorrow at eleven."

7

As soon as Gavin Davis had left, Brittany practically exploded with excitement, jumping up and down and squealing. "Oh, I'm so glad I came here! We get to go on Gavin Davis's yacht! This is so exciting! I can't wait until tomorrow!"

The others all stared at her in astonishment.

Brittany giggled. "I can't believe you all, pretending to be so cool about it!"

"Well, I'm not pretending," Lauren replied. "And I'm kind of surprised that *you're* so excited, after what you said about sailing being so boring."

For once, Jody detected an edge of impatience in Lauren's normally friendly manner toward Brittany.

"This is completely different," Brittany said. She rolled her eyes. "Gavin Davis isn't going to have some dinky little sailboat — he's a multimillionaire! Don't you know who he is?"

"It looks like none of us do," said Jerry. "So why don't you tell us?" he suggested.

Brittany took a deep breath. "They call him the 'Biz Whiz,'" she began. "There was a story about him in *People* magazine a few months ago, and he's been on the cover of *Business Week*. My mom says he's a financial genius."

"What does he do?" Jerry asked.

Brittany shrugged. "Well, I don't know, exactly. But it said in *People* magazine that he'd made a fortune by helping to save businesses that were on the brink of disaster. They said that everything he touches turns to gold."

Jody noticed that Jerry had gone rather pale. "I think I want to go inside and sit down," he said in a faint voice. "I can't believe I nearly told him to go away. People pay that man lots and lots of money to sort out their business problems. And he's just offered to help CETA for free!"

June 29 — evening.
Have been invited to spend tomorrow on the Davises'
yacht — turns out Mr. Davis is a millionaire and is going to
help CETA! Couldn't believe it when Brittany insisted on
calling Mom on Dolphin Dreamer *to ask her to bring more*
of her clothes back so she could find something good
enough to wear for the occasion! I just know she is going
to gush and giggle all over the place. How embarrassing!

It was another typical beautiful hot summer Florida day as Jody and the others waited on the dock of the bay for the promised motorboat. Craig and Gina had decided to stay at CETA to help Bud with some heavy maintenance work that needed to be done, and the twins voted for another day out the bicycles. But besides Lauren and Brittany, Maddie had accepted the invitation. And soon afterward, so had Cam. Jody guessed that he really just wanted the chance to spend more time with Maddie, who was looking especially great in a short orange skirt and midriff top.

After trying and rejecting practically everything in her wardrobe, Brittany was wearing a white sundress, and had gotten Lauren to help pin up her hair.

Jody felt very plain by comparison in shorts and T-shirt, and was glad that Lauren had also chosen to stay casual in her usual cutoff jeans and sleeveless shirt. Brittany had urged Lauren to dress up, but Jody had heard Lauren calmly but firmly declare that she preferred comfort to fashion. Perhaps Lauren had started to realize that she and Brittany didn't really have very much in common, after all.

Soon a motorboat came roaring through the lagoon and pulled up to the dock.

The handsome, black-haired young man at the wheel identified himself as Rob Holdstock, of the yacht *Daisy Mae*. "Gavin apologizes for not coming along, but he wasn't sure how many passengers there would be," he explained. "I thought I might have to make two trips, but I can see that won't be necessary. Can I give you a hand getting on, Miss?" he asked with an admiring look at Maddie.

"That won't be necessary," said Cam jealously. Then, blushing, as Maddie shot him an amused glance, he added, "I mean, there's no need for you to get out; I'll make sure everyone boards safely."

When Gavin Davis had spoken about his "yacht," Jody had imagined something about the size of *Dolphin Dreamer*, a boat that would be perfectly com-

The Daisy Mae

fortable for a family of three plus a small crew to spend their vacations on. The reality took her by surprise. *Daisy Mae* was enormous.

Cam whistled through his teeth as the large, luxurious yacht came into sight, just beyond the lagoon. "Wow," he said, scratching his blond head in amazement.

"It looks like an ocean liner compared to what we're used to," Maddie said.

"It's my idea of what a yacht should be," Brittany sighed, her face glowing with excitement.

Janet and Gavin Davis welcomed them on board, smiling broadly and looking genuinely pleased to see them. Janet wore a gauzy, sea-green dress, but her husband was casually dressed in faded cutoffs and a Miami Dolphins T-shirt.

"Where's little Hal?" Lauren asked.

Janet smoothed her hair back from her face. "He's watching TV," she said with a sigh. "I tried to get him interested in coming out to say hello, but . . ."

"He'll come out once we're moving," Gavin said. "Hal likes it best when the boat is moving," he explained.

"Come on, I'll give you the grand tour," said Janet, including them all in her smile. "Follow me."

Inside, *Daisy Mae* was more like a luxurious hotel than a boat. The cabins were all so large, and so lavishly furnished, that Jody found herself thinking of them as rooms. It was staffed like a hotel, too, with two chefs working in a large, gleaming kitchen. "What would Mei Lin think of this?" she whispered to Maddie, who grinned back.

There was a "grand cabin" and a "small cabin" and even a room devoted to television viewing, furnished with the most up-to-date equipment, its walls lined with videotapes and DVDs.

Hal, absorbed in an episode of *Thomas the Tank Engine*, didn't show any sign of noticing that he had company when Janet led them in.

"Hal, when this one is over, it's time for lunch," Janet said, speaking to her son in a clear voice. "I'll come back to tell you then."

The boy did not move, speak, or interrupt his viewing in any way.

"Did he hear you?" Maddie asked.

"I'm not sure if he notices anything else when he's that absorbed in something," Janet replied. "But I have to keep trying. I'll come back in five minutes and try again, but he's probably going to start screaming when I switch the set off."

Lunch was delicious and lavish. Everything had been laid out on the long table in the grand cabin, and everyone was invited to load up a plate and take it out to eat on deck.

"Wow, these are some picnic plates, huh?" Lauren rolled her eyes and pointed to the gleaming white, gold-edged china.

Jody returned her grin as she began scooping up portions of fresh shrimp, barbecued ribs, potato salad, coleslaw, guacamole, tortilla chips, and garlic bread. Soon her plate was full — though she hadn't sampled half of what was offered. She picked up some silver cutlery and one of the crisp, white linen napkins.

Chairs had been set out under the shade of an

awning on deck, and there was a choice of cold drinks in a cooler.

After she'd eaten all she could, Jody went up for a stroll on the forward deck. Up there, she could feel how swiftly they were moving. As she paused to look over the side, she saw something that made her heart pound faster: a group of dolphins was riding the bow-wave created as *Daisy Mae* cut through the water.

There were five or six of the sleek, gray animals, leaping and diving, bumping against one another playfully as they jostled for the best position. Her eyes swept over them, searching for distinctive differences. Bottle-nosed dolphins all tended to look very much the same, especially from a distance. Then she caught her breath as she saw the bright blue plastic tag in one dorsal fin.

"Hermes!" she breathed. There could be no doubt about it. There was the plastic dart with the micro-transmitter that Jefferson Taylor had fired into one of Apollo's group.

So where was Apollo? Eagerly, she scanned the leaping dolphins, searching for her special friend. But there were only six dolphins in the water. Mentally, she identified each one, and neither Rosie nor Apollo was among them.

As she frowned and chewed her lip in dismay, Jody was joined at the rail by Janet and Hal, Lauren, and Brittany.

"Oh, that breeze feels great," Lauren exclaimed. Then she caught sight of the dolphins and gasped.

Everyone else seemed to notice the dolphins at the same time, including Hal, who gave a wordless cry and reached out with both hands.

Jody was glad to see his mother had a firm grip on him. She really didn't like the idea of having to test her lifesaving skills in deep water, for real!

"Are those the dolphins you were looking for?" Janet asked.

Lauren had been leaning over the side for a better look. Now she drew back, disappointment plain on her face. "No," she replied flatly. "Rosie's not there."

"Neither is Apollo," Jody told her.

"So you think Rosie might be with Apollo?" Lauren asked.

Jody nodded, gazing sympathetically into Lauren's worried face.

"Here comes another one," Brittany called out. "Look, Lauren, is that Rosie?"

Lauren turned eagerly back to look, shading her eyes against the sun. Almost immediately, she shook her head.

But Jody recognized the solitary dolphin. "It's Apollo!" she cried joyfully.

In response, Apollo reared up out of the water, clicking and chattering urgently.

"It's almost like he's trying to tell you something," said Janet Davis in surprise.

Jody leaned over the side, longing to be closer to Apollo. He was clacking his jaw in a way she hadn't seen before, moving his body back and forth and whistling loudly. "What is it?" she murmured. She could sense his distress.

"It must be about Rosie," Lauren said, giving words to Jody's feeling. "She isn't with him, or with the others. There must be something wrong, and he's come to tell us!"

Now, seeming to give up trying to make Jody understand, Apollo dived underwater again, throwing himself against Poseidon to get the big dolphin's attention.

Gradually, all the dolphins stopped their joyful play and began to swim around Apollo in a tight circle.

Jody and the others watching from the boat could hear a lot of rapid clicking, whistling, and other sounds, as if the dolphins were having a furious discussion. Then, as if they'd all agreed, they suddenly shot off in a group, moving rapidly away.

Hal gave a disappointed cry.

Jody felt exactly the same way. To her surprise, the lead dolphin — it was Apollo — suddenly broke away from the group and raced back to the side of the boat. He rose up out of the water, making another series of loud, sharp clicks, before swimming back to his group.

This time, Jody had no doubt about what he meant.

"What's going on up here?" Gavin Davis's friendly voice sounded behind her.

Jody turned to look at him. "Apollo wants us to follow him," she said. "I think there's something wrong, and he came to get his friends — and us — to help. Can we go after them? Please?" She held her breath waiting for his answer.

He gazed at her keenly. It was obvious he understood how important this was to her. "Of course," he said at once. "I'll go and give the order to follow that dolphin!"

8

For a while, all went smoothly as *Daisy Mae* easily followed in the wake of the dolphins. Maddie and Cam joined Jody and the others at the rail of the foredeck, where they all shared the excitement.

After about ten minutes, a line of coast came in sight, and as the dolphins raced ahead into a rounded bay, the big yacht slowed and hung back.

"What's wrong?" Jody asked as they came to a stop. "We're going to lose them!"

As the dolphins vanished from sight, Hal began to

moan. He jerked away and hugged himself when his mother tried to comfort him.

Rob Holdstock came dashing up to Gavin Davis. "I'm sorry, sir," he said breathlessly. "Captain says we can't go any closer without running aground. It's very shallow here, and there's a sandbank marked on the chart."

"Does that mean we've lost them?" Lauren asked.

Jody bit her lip in dismay.

Gavin Davis glanced at the girls' anxious faces, but spoke to Rob. "Where are we?"

"Just beside an uninhabited key. No name given for it on the navigation chart," Rob replied.

Jody looked over the side, trying to judge the distance to the shore. It was a calm day, and she thought she'd swim it easily. Depending on where the sandbank started, she reasoned that she could probably walk more than half the way.

She looked around at Gavin Davis again, and made her suggestion. "I could swim over and find out where the dolphins have gone."

"Oh, there's no need to swim," he said. "Rob can take

you in the motorboat. That way, if you find anything wrong, you can phone us for help."

They quickly got ready to go. Maddie said she would go along, and Cam seconded her. Jody was surprised when Brittany announced that she was coming, too, since she'd seemed so at home on the yacht. But maybe she felt a bit shy without the other girls around, especially since Janet Davis was now too busy looking after Hal to pay much attention to her.

Soon after they left the yacht in the motorboat Apollo reappeared, leaping out of the water and making a lot of noise to make sure he had their attention.

Jody grinned. "We see you, Apollo!" she yelled. "We're coming!"

"What does he want with us?" Cam wondered, scratching his head. "Isn't it pretty strange for a wild animal to act like that?"

"I've heard stories of wild dolphins approaching complete strangers when they've needed help," Maddie said. "Dolphins have been known to help people in distress — like Apollo rescuing Jody when she fell overboard. Since they help us, maybe they figure we will help them. And, of course, we're not strangers to Apollo."

"I'm sure Apollo knows I'd do anything to help him," Jody said fervently.

"Yeah, but there doesn't seem to be anything wrong with him," Cam pointed out.

"No, he must want our help for someone, or something, else," Maddie concluded.

"I think we're about to find out the answer," said Rob, raising his voice above the roar of the engine. "Look, the dolphins are all together there in the bay. End of the line, folks," He switched off the engine, and peace descended.

They'd come to the sandbank. "You can wade to shore from here," Rob pointed out.

Kicking off her shoes, Jody was the first to leap out of the motorboat and onto the sandbank. There, the shallow warm water rose only to her ankles. A few yards away, the sandbank dropped again to form a slightly deeper pool where the dolphins all were.

"Are they trapped?" asked Lauren, concerned, splashing up behind her.

Jody shook her head. "I don't think so, but . . ." She was puzzled to know how the dolphins had gotten to where they were — until she noticed that the sandbank was not quite the total barrier it had seemed at first. One of the dolphins was swimming back and forth at the other side of the bay, between the shallow pool and the open sea. There the sandbank dropped away to form a narrow channel that the dolphins were using as a passage. They could easily get in and out. So what was the problem?

Maddie and Cam waded out to join Jody and Lauren, but Brittany announced that she didn't want to get her dress wet, so would stay in the boat with Rob.

"Give us a yell if you need any help," he told them.

Jody nodded distractedly, staring at the dolphins and trying to figure it out. The scene was idyllic: a curving half-moon of gleaming white sandy beach, brilliant blue water reflecting back a clear blue sky, and a group of dolphins frolicking in the shallow bay. Except these dolphins weren't playing. They were swimming rapidly back and forth in a worried way, and their whistles and clicks didn't sound happy to Jody.

She shook her head as she waded forward, going to meet Apollo. "What's wrong?" she muttered to herself.

"Just that big pile of garbage somebody dumped," Lauren answered, her voice disgusted. "I just hate the way some people dump all their litter on the keys where nobody lives. Look at that."

Jody followed Lauren's pointing finger and noticed the heap of sodden cardboard boxes, newspapers, empty cans, plastic bags, and other junk at the edge of the beach and spilling over into the water. Some green plastic bottles bobbed about, and there was a heap of bright blue netting tangled up with something. . . . At first Jody thought it was a dark gray plastic bag, more unwanted rubbish, but then she realized what she was looking at, and gasped, "It's a dolphin, trapped in all of that junk!"

Both girls broke into a run, pounding through the water that became first knee- and then thigh-deep.

As they came nearer, Jody could see that it was definitely a dolphin that had become tangled in the dumped netting, and that the animal was lying frighteningly still in the shallow water.

121

Jody hoped they had arrived in time to help.

Lauren got there just ahead of her, and crouched down in the water. "It's Rosie," she reported breathlessly. "And she's still breathing, thank goodness! Oh, Rosie, my poor darling," Lauren went on, a catch in her voice. "Let me get this horrible stuff off of you!"

"I'll help," Jody offered. Both girls tried tugging gently at the plastic netting, but it was hard to even loosen it. In places the netting was wound so tightly around Rosie that it dug deep into her skin.

"She must have been struggling to get away, and just got herself tangled up even more," Lauren said. "Oh, Rosie, Rosie!" She was crying.

Tears came to Jody's eyes as well, but she blinked them away. "Just hang on, we're going to get you out of it," she promised. "Lauren, I think we're going to have to cut the net to set her free."

Cam and Maddie had just splashed up to join them. "I've got a knife," said Cam, unhooking the bulky Swiss Army knife from his belt.

"If that has a scissors attachment it might be better — safer," Maddie suggested. "Do you want me to do it?"

At Cam's nod, she found the small scissors and carefully set to work.

Lauren unwrapped a strand from Rosie's jaw, talking in a low, soothing voice all the while, and Maddie clipped away the tightly wound netting from her body and tail. Although she longed to help, Jody kept back, out of the way.

Within a few minutes, it was done. Rosie was free.

But she didn't move. Her eyes were open, and Jody could see the gentle movement of her blowhole as she breathed, but the dolphin didn't even try to swim away.

Lauren stroked Rosie's sides, careful not to hurt her. The net had left many welts, and she was bleeding from several cuts, including one very deep one in her fin. "Come on, sweetie," Lauren said softly. "It's okay to move now. That nasty old net is gone — there's nothing to tangle you up now. Why won't you try to move?"

Rosie did not respond. Lauren bit her lip. Jody could see she was battling against tears.

"Maybe we should call your folks and ask them what to do," Jody suggested.

Lauren nodded, looking more hopeful.

"Rob has a phone on the motorboat," Maddie reminded them. "I'll run back. I can call them, if you like, tell them where we are, and ask them to phone the vet."

"Thanks, Maddie," Lauren said gratefully. "I'd really like to stay here with Rosie."

"I'm sure that's the very best thing you can do for her," Maddie agreed. "You keep her comfortable, tell her everything's going to be all right, and hang on till your folks get here."

Maddie and Cam waded back to the motorboat where Rob and Brittany were waiting. Not wanting to disturb Lauren's quiet communication with Rosie, Jody moved away a little, into the warm, shallow water of the natural pool. She looked at the wild dolphins who were still swimming back and forth through the channel, whistling and clicking to one another. Jody thought they must be calling to Rosie, too, and it was even more worrying that the injured dolphin did not reply.

Apollo came gliding through the water and rubbed against Jody's legs. She smiled at the feel of his smooth skin against hers. Looking down, she met his eye. As always, there was a feeling of connection when their gaze met, and she felt calmer. Apollo made her feel peaceful, as if everything was going to be all right.

After about a quarter of an hour, Jody could hear the sound of motorboats approaching. A few minutes later, two boats came into view. Jody recognized Alice and Jerry in *Princess*. The second boat bore the letters "D.O.B." as its name, and was driven by a sturdy, dark-haired, middle-aged woman. Leaving the boat, she came splashing through the shallows with a medical bag in one hand.

"Maria Gomez," she identified herself briskly as she approached Jody. "I'm the vet. Now, what seems to be . . . my goodness, this isn't Rosie!" The woman looked in surprise at Apollo, who was still swimming around Jody's legs.

"No," Jody agreed. "This is Apollo, and there's nothing wrong with him! Rosie's over there, with Lauren." She half turned and pointed to where Lauren was crouched in the water with Rosie.

Maria Gomez looked puzzled. "Apollo? I haven't met him before."

"He's a wild dolphin," Jody explained. She saw Alice approaching, a worried look on her face. Jerry, moving a little more slowly and carrying a bucket of fish, was not far behind. Jody continued, "It was Apollo who led us to Rosie."

The vet's eyes widened. "I want to hear all about it — later," she said. "But now I'd better go see about Rosie."

"How is she?" Alice asked anxiously as she hurried up.

"She's alive," Jody assured her. "And we can't see any really deep cuts or anything, just little ones, but she just seems worn out. Lauren can't get her to swim at all. We think maybe she was struggling to get out of the net for a long time and just used up her strength."

Alice sighed. "Hopefully Maria can tell us more when she's examined her."

The vet was talking to Lauren and squatting in the shallow water to run her hands all over the injured dolphin as she listened to what the girl had to tell her.

Apollo had decided to swim away with the arrival of

Alice and Jerry. Happy to have Jody's company in the shallow pool, he'd obviously decided there were too many people around for his comfort. Jody watched him swim over to join his friends on the other side of the sandbank, then turned as she heard Jerry speaking to her.

"Your folks stayed behind to look after the twins and hold down the fort for us," he explained. "I still had one more patient to see this afternoon, but Kim convinced me she can handle him herself," Jerry went on, rubbing his face with his free hand. "I was too worried about Rosie to wait behind," he added. "I care about her almost as if she were my child!"

The vet finished her examination and beckoned Jerry to approach. Jody followed.

"I can't find anything seriously wrong with her," Maria Gomez said, a slight frown creasing her forehead in concentration. "It's my guess that her problem is shock and exhaustion. The whole situation must have been pretty traumatic for her, poor thing. Trapped and in pain, far from her own home and family. And if she's been struggling against that net for most of a day and night she's probably starving, too." She looked around. "Where's that fish?"

"Right here," said Jerry, stepping forward with the bucket. "And there's another just like this in the boat!"

"Good." Maria Gomez nodded her dark head approvingly. She looked at Lauren. "Rosie probably knows and trusts you better than anyone else. You try hand-feeding her. Maybe after she gets some fish in her belly she'll start acting more like her old self."

Lauren nodded seriously. Taking the bucket from her father, she looked at Jody. "Want to help me, Jody?"

"Sure!" Jody rushed forward, eager to help.

Rosie was lying still in the shallow water, in the same position as before. Only the brightness of her eyes, and the faint motion of her blowhole as she breathed, showed that she was alive.

"Got a treat for you, sweetie," said Lauren in a low, musical voice. She waved a fish in front of Rosie's beak. "Open wide!"

For a moment it seemed the dolphin would not respond. Jody held her breath.

Then, with a faint creaking sound, Rosie's jaws

parted. Lauren dropped in the fish. "Good girl! Want another?"

Rosie definitely did. This time, she opened her mouth as soon as the fish appeared.

Gradually, she began to perk up, and was soon eating greedily.

The vet's pager began to beep and she apologized for having to rush away on another emergency. "As far as I can see, your dolphin is on the mend. Give her all she wants to eat, and try to coax her to swim. If she doesn't seem much better by the evening, give me a call and I'll come back, all right?"

Alice and Jerry agreed, and thanked her for coming so swiftly. They began to walk her back to her boat. "I can see I'm going to need that second bucket of fish after all," Jerry said with a grin.

Now, Lauren and Jody took turns feeding Rosie. Shortly after the vet's motorboat roared away, Jody heard another motor and looked up to see that the motorboat from the *Daisy Mae* had gone.

Returning with the bucket of fish carried between them, Alice and Jerry explained that Rob had gone back to pick up the Davises. "They're eager to see Rosie, and I know he wants me to have a look at his boy," Jerry said. He shrugged. "I think I owe him that much for helping us to find Rosie! Maria thought that since Rosie is physically okay, and is used to meeting people, it would do no harm."

Rosie chomped her way through most of the second bucket of fish before deciding she'd had enough.

"There's nothing wrong with her appetite," Jerry said cheerfully.

"Maybe after she's had a little rest she'll feel like a swim," Alice said hopefully.

The motorboat from the *Daisy Mae* returned carrying Janet, Hal, and Gavin Davis, as well as Brittany, all wearing swimsuits. Jody noticed that Hal also wore a life jacket — obviously this time his mother had decided to take no chances, even in the shallowest water.

And she was right to be worried. As soon as they were out of the boat, Hal was struggling to pull away from his parents' restraining hands, his eyes fixed on the deeper water beyond the sandbar, grunting wordlessly as he tried to fling himself into it.

"We're going into the water together, Hal," his mother said loudly. "You must stay close to Mommy and Daddy."

He kept struggling and grunting as if she hadn't spoken.

Jody felt sorry for both parents and child, who couldn't seem to communicate. She began to walk toward the little boy, trying to get his attention. "Look at the dolphin, Hal," she said. "This is Rosie."

Rosie meets Hal

Whether her words had gotten through, or he'd just happened to notice the animal lying in the shallow water, Jody didn't know. But when he finally saw Rosie, a change came over Hal. Suddenly, he became quiet. He stopped struggling and simply stared. Then he said, "What's wrong?"

Janet Davis gasped.

Jody was amazed. Short as it was, this was the first clear sentence she'd ever heard the little boy speak. Slowly and carefully, Jody told him, "Rosie got caught in a net and couldn't get out. We helped her get free, but I think she's still kind of tired."

"Tired," the boy echoed. Still staring intently at the resting dolphin he asked, "Go sleep?"

"No, she's awake," Jody said.

"Play with Hal?" Again, the boy seemed to speak more to the dolphin than to Jody, even though she was right in front of him.

Jody looked questioningly at Hal's parents and found that they were looking to Jerry for the answer.

Jerry Rozakis nodded. He waded into the water and stood directly in front of Hal. Then he crouched,

132

putting himself on a level with the boy, and spoke directly to him. "Rosie is a friendly dolphin. She's not feeling too well right now, but maybe you can make her feel better, Hal. You can go into the water with Rosie, but you must listen to the grown-ups, and do what we tell you. Nod your head if you understand me."

For a moment, as Hal went on gazing beyond Jerry at the dolphin, Jody was afraid he hadn't heard, or that he would act as if he hadn't heard. But after a second's delay he nodded.

"Good boy," said Jerry approvingly. "You must keep your life jacket on while you're in the water, and you must always have two people with you. You choose who you want to be with you, Hal."

Expecting the little boy to choose his parents, or maybe Jerry, Jody was astonished when Hal pointed his finger at her, and then at Lauren.

"Jody and Lauren," Jerry said. "That's fine. Remember to do what they say. If you don't, you'll have to come out. Now Jody and Lauren will take you to meet Rosie."

9

Standing on either side of Hal, Lauren and Jody walked him off the sandbank and into the slightly deeper water. As they went, Lauren kept up a soothing stream of talk. "Now we'll just go splash, splash through this water here until we come to Rosie. Look, she's watching us! See her eye, there? She may be still, but she's awake. She's wondering who you are, Hal. She knows me and Jody, but she hasn't met you before, has she? She doesn't know you."

"Hal," said the boy.

"Yes, that's right," Lauren agreed. "You're Hal, and this is Rosie."

"Rosie," he repeated, staring intently as they brought him close to the animal resting in the shallows near the shore.

"Do you want to touch her, Hal?" Lauren asked in a gentle voice. "You can stroke Rosie if you like."

Jody demonstrated by running the palm of her hand firmly along Rosie's flank.

Hal nodded. Moving stiffly, he stretched out one hand. After a moment's hesitation, he brought his hand down through the water to rest on Rosie's side. Then, slowly and gently, he began to stroke her.

Jody stood in silence, watching. The sun beat down on her head, and the air was still except for the hum of a few insects and the endless ebb and swell of the sea beyond the quiet little bay. She felt that she was witnessing a minor miracle, as this isolated little boy made contact with another creature.

"You can talk to her, you know." Lauren made the suggestion as she watched him stroking Rosie. "You

Best of friends!

can talk to her while you're touching her — she'd like that. Would you like to try it?"

Hal went on patting the dolphin, showing no sign that he had heard what Lauren said. Then suddenly, unexpectedly, he nodded. And then, to Jody's astonishment, he opened his mouth and made a sound like a creaky hinge — an excellent imitation of a dolphin sound!

Although Rosie had not made a sound since they'd found her, Hal had obviously remembered hearing this noise from Apollo or some of the other wild dolphins he had watched from the yacht.

Then Jody was even more amazed. Rosie responded. She moved a little, and poked her beak out of the water. Hal walked toward her head and peered down at her eye. He made the creaking noise again, a little louder this time.

Rosie creaked right back at him!

Jody looked at Lauren. Her eyes were wide with astonishment — she looked as stunned as Jody felt. Their eyes met and they grinned happily at each other.

Hal showed no sign of happiness or excitement. He looked as stiff and solemn as ever. But he stroked

Rosie's beak and made the creaking noise again. When she gave out a string of rapid-fire clicks, he tried his best to imitate them.

From behind her, Jody heard Hal's mother give a stifled cry. In tones of wonder, Gavin Davis said, "He's actually trying to talk to that animal."

Suddenly, Rosie flexed her tail. A moment later, she was gliding through the water between Jody and Hal, rubbing against their bare legs. She swam in a circle around the three of them, poking her beak out of the water to make creaking and clicking noises in the air.

Hal followed every move the dolphin made, watching her intently. When she rolled onto her back, offering her belly, he seemed to understand at once that she was asking to be stroked.

Gradually, as he responded to Rosie, Hal's expression began to change. His whole body relaxed. The terrible, stiff blankness of his face became peaceful.

Jody was thrilled. Through some sort of animal magic, Rosie was able to reach Hal as no person could. And by concentrating on reaching the boy, Rosie was healing herself at the same time. It was wonderful.

Far too soon, it seemed to them all, Jerry called time.

Hal started to get upset, making the strange wordless groans that Jody had heard before.

But Jerry was right there, his hands on the boy's shoulders, his piercing eyes commanding attention. "Hal," he said firmly. "Rosie needs to rest. She's had a bad time. You've helped her feel better but she needs to rest now. You can come and see her again tomorrow, if you like, but you have to be good. That means no fussing. Go with your parents, do what they tell you, and they'll bring you back tomorrow."

The groaning stopped. Hal stared into Jerry's eyes, saw that he meant it, and nodded.

Gavin Davis seemed less sure. "You really mean it?" he asked Jerry.

"Of course." Jerry gestured around at the little bay. "I don't mean *here,* though. Rosie seems to be okay now, so I think we can get her back to CETA all right. Come there, tomorrow. Five o'clock? Stay and have dinner with us afterward, if you don't mind potluck."

"That's very kind of you," Gavin Davis said slowly.

"But I know you're overworked already. I don't want to put you under more pressure, just because —"

"Don't worry about it," Jerry cut him off. "I can't offer you my full professional services, but if you're happy for Hal to be looked after by my two talented young assistants . . ." He gestured at Jody and Lauren.

Feeling herself blush, Jody concentrated on watching Rosie, who was swimming idly around the small bay.

"I'm sure Hal wouldn't want anyone else," Gavin Davis said warmly. "No one could have done a better job than they have today."

Jody glowed with happiness. She couldn't believe how lucky she was, to be allowed to work with dolphins this way. She exchanged a glance with Lauren and saw that the other girl was looking thrilled, too.

Everyone said their good-byes, and the Davises headed back on their motorboat for the *Daisy Mae*, taking Maddie and Cam with them. While Lauren and Jody had been busy with Hal and Rosie, Cam had managed to convince Maddie to let him show her the sights of Key West that evening.

"Tell your folks I may be back late," Maddie told Jody, smiling broadly.

"And that I've promised to take good care of their assistant," Cam added with a wink. He looked very pleased with himself Jody thought as she waved good-bye.

"What's going to happen to Rosie?" Brittany asked Alice Rozakis as she climbed on board *Princess*.

"We're hoping she'll follow us back to CETA," Alice said quietly, exchanging a glance with her husband.

"She certainly seems to have recovered," Jerry said, shading his eyes as he gazed out to where Rosie was now playing with the wild dolphins. He added, "We're only a few miles from Cedar Key. I don't think such a short journey will wear her out, but you girls can keep an eye on her. If she seems to be flagging at all, I'll slow down."

"You can count on us," said Lauren. Now that she realized Rosie was okay, Lauren had recovered her usual calm, cheerful good nature.

Not wanting to upset her, Jody didn't mention what she was thinking: What if Rosie decided to stay with her newfound friends in the wild, rather than return to her old life at CETA?

However, as soon as *Princess* began to motor away from the sandbank, Rosie came leaping through the water to follow the boat.

Jody, Lauren, and Brittany all leaned over the back to watch her, but Rosie was not content to stay behind. As if to prove how fit she was, the dolphin shot through the water, streaking past the motorboat and then returning to leap in and out of the water on either side of the prow.

Laughing with delight, Lauren called to her father, "I think she wants us to go faster! She's looking for a wave to ride!"

"I think you're right," Jerry agreed. He was laughing, too.

Jody could see that Rosie's recovery had lifted a great weight of worry off his shoulders.

"Okay, girls, hang on!" The engine roared as he powered it up. As the boat cut through the water it created a foam-crested wave that Rosie rode. Soon the other dolphins joined in, butting and jostling each other for the best place.

After about ten minutes, Jody recognized the familiar buildings of CETA and realized they were approaching Cedar Key.

Jerry slowed the boat. The dolphins began to drop away. Apollo poked his nose up out of the water near the back of the boat and looked at Jody. He made his creaking sound.

Jody reached out her hand and briefly touched his nose. "See you later?" she said hopefully.

The dolphin butted her hand and gave a series of chattering clicks in reply before diving down and swimming away after the rest of his group.

Now, only Rosie remained beside the boat. She pushed her beak out of the water and looked at them.

Alice picked up the cell phone as Jerry idled the motor. "I'm going to call the office and get Kim to open the sea gate," she explained as she punched the buttons. "It looks like Rosie is ready to come home."

Sure enough, Jody saw that Rosie was speeding

through the water toward the fence. They could hear her whistling and clicking, and, moments later, there was a response from the dolphins on the inside.

Alice got through to Kim and quickly explained the situation. "See you in a few minutes," she promised. Breaking the connection, she exchanged a relieved smile with her husband. "Thank goodness this has all ended so happily," she said with a small sigh.

Jerry nodded. "Shall I take the boat around to the dock?" he suggested.

"Can we wait to see the gates open, and Rosie go in?" Lauren asked. She was peering toward the gate with a slight frown.

"Okay," her father agreed, smiling. Then his smile faded. "I can't see her, though, can you?"

They all looked. They could still hear the faint, excited sounds of dolphins, and the familiar shape of the bottle-nosed beaks on the other side of the fence, but there was no sign of Rosie.

"She's probably just underwater," Alice said when a splashing sound drew their attention to the side of the boat.

They just caught sight of a curved dorsal fin and a flip of the tail as Rosie surfaced just long enough to take a breath before shooting away underwater — away from the boat, away from them, away from CETA.

"Rosie!" Lauren cried out in anguish. "Please come back! Please!" She turned to her parents. "Do you think she thought she was locked out?"

With a metallic shriek, the sea gate creaked open. Looking toward CETA, Jody saw her dad and Kim waving at them.

"She'll have heard that, surely," Alice said.

They all gazed in the direction Rosie had gone, waiting for her to return, hoping against hope. But the minutes ticked past without Rosie.

Finally, Jerry called an end to their wait by starting the engine.

"Oh, Daddy, please, just a little longer." Lauren begged.

"Sweetheart, Rosie will either come back, or she won't. Our being here doesn't make any difference. And I can't hang around on the water all day — I've got work to do," Jerry added, sounding weary.

Lauren looked close to tears. Jody knew how she felt, but could think of no comfort to offer.

Dinner that evening was a gloomy meal, even though Alice pointed out that the important thing was that they knew Rosie was well and happy.

"We've always known that some day she would probably want to live in the wild — it's just happened a little sooner than we'd expected," she reminded them quietly.

Lauren nodded sadly, pushing mashed potatoes around her plate. Then she looked up at her father. "Could we leave the sea gates open tonight, just in case she comes back?"

"Oh, no," Jerry said. "Absolutely not! The way my luck is running, the other three would decide to swim out and never come back! I'm sorry, sweetheart. But Rosie's made her choice; she's not going to come back now."

"Anyway, she could jump over the fence if she wanted to," Sean said suddenly. "Dolphins can jump really high. I know — I've seen them."

Jody stared across the table at her little brother. "Yeah, so have I," she said slowly, thinking about it. "I'm sure I've seen Apollo jump higher — much higher — than that fence. So how come your dolphins don't jump over it? Why do you need a gate at all?"

"I guess they could if they really wanted to," Alice said. "But they never have."

"Yes, it's odd, but although dolphins can be trained to leap over things, you'll almost never see a wild dolphin jump over any kind of barrier," Gina agreed. "No one knows why, but if a dolphin can't swim under, through, or around something, they act as if they *can't* jump over it. So even a very low fence will keep them in one place."

"That's weird," said Jimmy.

"May I be excused?" Lauren said quietly. "I'm not very hungry."

"Yes, of course, sweetheart," said her mother, giving her a concerned look.

"Me, neither," said Brittany, pushing aside her plate.

Jody watched unhappily as the two girls hurried away together.

June 30 — evening.
I hope Lauren doesn't blame me for losing Rosie, but I

*wouldn't be surprised if she does. If Apollo hadn't fol-
lowed us here, Rosie would still be living happily at CETA
with her mother.*

*I felt so close to Lauren when we rescued Rosie, but
now I feel like I'm just in the way. Maybe Brittany can
cheer her up. I wish*

Jody broke off and shut her diary hastily as the bedroom door opened. Lauren came in with Brittany right
behind her.

"Okay, if we're not going to watch TV, let's put some
music on," Brittany said. Ignoring Jody, she marched
across the room to Lauren's stereo and began to go
through her CD collection. "What do you feel like?"

"I don't feel like listening to music right now," Lauren
said quietly. "I'm going to take a bath and go to bed."

"It's too early to go to bed," Brittany objected, scowl-
ing.

"Well, I'm tired," Lauren said.

"You can't be, not yet," Brittany said crossly.

Jody stood up. "Come on, Brittany," she said firmly.
"Let's leave Lauren in peace."

Brittany turned on her. "Be quiet," she snapped. "Lauren's my friend, not yours!"

"If you were really Lauren's friend, you'd do what she wants, instead of just thinking about yourself," Jody replied fiercely.

"I'm more important than some silly animal," Brittany shouted, her face turning red. She glared at Lauren. "I thought you were different at first, but you're as bad as *she* is." She tossed her head to indicate Jody. "Just another boring dolphin fanatic! Why did I ever waste my time on somebody who thinks it matters on which side of a fence some stupid dolphin wants to live! You two were just *made* for each other!" Then she stormed out of the bedroom.

Lauren's eyes were wide. After a moment she turned to Jody and spoke. "You don't look surprised. Have you seen her like that before?"

Jody nodded.

Lauren looked thoughtful. "I don't suppose there's any chance that *she* might decide she'd rather go live in the wild instead of staying with us?"

10

Next morning, Jody and Lauren breathed a sigh of relief when Brittany demanded to be taken back to *Dolphin Dreamer*. But they were still worried about how Hal Davis would react when he found Rosie wasn't there.

Jerry tried to reassure them. "He probably won't notice that it's a different dolphin. Bottle-nosed dolphins look so much alike that even experts can find it hard to tell them apart."

"But Rosie has that scar over her eye," Lauren pointed out. "It's pretty distinctive."

"Well . . ." Her father shrugged uneasily. "All right, he

might notice the difference, but as long as he's allowed to get into the water and play with a dolphin, I'd be amazed if he made a fuss about which one. None of the other children have minded."

"I guess you're right," said Lauren. "Which one should it be?"

"Take your pick," Jerry told the girls. "They're all free. I'll be in the office, having a conference with some parents to discuss ways of teaching their child at home. I'm sure you'll do fine, but give me a yell if you need any help."

Jody and Lauren looked at each other when Jerry had gone. After a brief discussion they decided on Nora, who was also female, and the nearest in age to Rosie. They decided they wouldn't say anything about the change unless Hal asked. Once he got to know Nora they were sure he'd be fine, but if they warned him beforehand that Rosie was missing, he might throw a tantrum.

The Davises arrived promptly at five o'clock. They looked happy and excited. Jody thought she had never seen the little boy looking quite so alert and friendly. Somehow, that made her feel worse than ever.

"Cheer up," said Gavin Davis, smiling at the two girls. Then he cocked his head quizzically. "Is there something wrong?"

"We're just worried in case we do something wrong," Lauren said hastily. She was blushing. "Even though I've watched my dad hundreds of times, I can't help feeling nervous. . . ."

The shadow of suspicion quickly cleared away. "You girls have nothing to worry about," he said firmly. "You were absolutely brilliant with Hal yesterday. And, anyway, I understand that Jerry says the dolphins are the teachers here, so you don't have to worry too much about keeping Hal's attention — that's up to Rosie! And after what we saw yesterday, I can't believe she'd let us down."

Jody gulped and smiled weakly. "Come on, Hal," she called to the little boy. "Let's just check your life jacket . . . then we'll go into the shallow pool with . . . uh, with the dolphin."

Although he was obviously excited, Hal waited patiently for the girls to tell him he was allowed to get into the water.

As soon as they had slipped into the water, Nora came swimming up to investigate.

Staring intently at the sleek gray shape beneath the water, Hal opened his mouth and made the same creaking nose he'd made the day before.

Nora poked her head out of the water to look at the boy.

Hal frowned. He leaned forward, staring intently. Jody held her breath and exchanged a glance with Lauren. Was he looking for Rosie's scar? He didn't say anything. After a moment, he made the creaking noise again.

Unlike Rosie, Nora didn't respond with sounds of her own. But at least she seemed interested in Hal, Jody thought.

"Do you want to give her a fish to eat, Hal?" Lauren suggested. She tapped her fingernails against the metal bucket beside the pool.

Hal didn't take his eyes off Nora.

"Dolphins love fish," Jody added. "Hal, she'd like it if you gave her a fish."

Hal ignored her, too. He made the creaking noise, paused, then tried again. It was as if he was alone in the pool with the dolphin.

Suddenly, he started to shake. "This dolphin's not my friend," he shouted. "I want my friend!"

Lauren and Jody exchanged a swift glance. "She *is* your friend, Hal," Lauren said urgently. "But she needs to get to know you. You're right that this isn't Rosie. This is one of Rosie's friends, and she wants to be friends with you, too. Her name is Nora."

"Rosie," Hal cried. "Rosie! Rosie! Rosie!" He paused, but it was only to draw breath to scream.

"What's wrong?" Alarmed by the screaming, Hal's mother peered down into the water at them.

"Hal!" Lauren spoke sharply. "Listen to me! If you don't calm down, you'll have to get out of the water this instant."

It got through to him. He stopped yelling. But now, Jody noticed in dismay, Nora was deserting them, swimming away out of the shallow pool, and making for the sea pen. She realized that Maxi and Nick were making an unusual amount of noise out there.

"I want Rosie," Hal said flatly.

Jody's heart sank. What could they say to him, how could they possibly control him now?

Lauren seemed to be thinking hard. Then, into the silence, came a dolphin's whistle. She turned in astonishment to gaze out toward the sea. "Rosie?" she cried.

"Rosie," Hal repeated. He threw his head back and began to make his creaking noise as loudly as he could. Then he paused. They all heard the whistle again. Hal tried to imitate it.

"It *is* Rosie. She's come back!" Lauren exclaimed. "Oh, Jody, please — can you manage Hal? I've got to open the sea gate before she leaves again!"

With that, Lauren hauled herself out of the shallow pool and went racing toward the storeroom where the controls were. Jody watched anxiously as her friend tried the door and discovered it was locked. She turned and ran toward the office.

Jody had her hands full trying to keep Hal under control. He was determined to fling himself further out into the water, seemingly drawn by the sound of Rosie's whistle.

Janet Davis slipped into the water, much to Jody's relief, and took charge of her son. "Hal, you have to do what the girls tell you, or they won't let you see Rosie," she said firmly. Then, frowning quizzically, she looked at Jody. "But I don't understand. Wasn't that Rosie in the pool with Hal? What's going on?"

Blushing, Jody told her what had happened. "I was afraid if we told Hal, he'd be too upset. . . . We hoped he wouldn't notice."

"Well, I couldn't tell the difference between them myself," Janet confessed. "But it's different for Hal. He really bonded with the one you call Rosie. Listen!" They both listened to the amazingly accurate whistle Hal was producing now. "It's eerie, isn't it? I would never have imagined he could do that. He sounds *exactly* like a dolphin," Janet said in wonder.

Lauren came running out of the office with her parents close behind. They were heading for the sea gate controls in the storeroom.

Before they reached the door, though, something happened that Jody knew she would never forget in her whole life.

Suddenly, Rosie came rising out of the water, her sleek body arching to make one fabulously high leap. It carried her straight over the fence, into the sea pen, where she splashed down, and disappeared beneath the water.

Jody gasped in astonishment.

"That dolphin just leaped over the fence!" Janet Davis exclaimed. "I had no idea they could jump that high!"

Rosie had yet another surprise in store.

As Jody stared in wonder, Rosie appeared, swimming through the narrow underwater passage that connected the shallow pool with the sea pens. She emerged into the shallow pool, swimming right up to Jody, Hal, and Janet, expelling a gust of air through her blowhole.

Hal began to click and whistle more urgently than ever. As soon as he paused for breath, Rosie replied with a long series of chattering clicks and trilling

Rosie returns!

whistles. If you closed your eyes, thought Jody, you wouldn't be able to tell from the sounds alone which came from the boy and which from the dolphin.

"I can't believe it," murmured Hal's mother. "It's like they're really talking to each other."

"They are," said Jody. She was suddenly sure of it, and she felt awed and moved by the obvious affection between them. "Rosie loves Hal. That's why she came back. Not just for her mother and Nick and Nora, but for the people at CETA as well. She thinks they're all part of her family." She turned as Lauren slipped into the water beside them.

Rosie broke off her conversation with Hal to swim up and butt gently against Lauren's legs.

"Yeah, I'm glad to see you, too, Rosie," said Lauren. There were tears on her cheeks, but she was smiling broadly as she slipped down into the water to hug the dolphin. "Welcome home!"

July 1 — bedtime.
We've been invited to spend the Fourth of July on board the Daisy Mae. *Gavin Davis has promised the most spec-*

tacular fireworks display we've ever seen. It will be a great celebration . . . and we have so many things to celebrate! It will also be a going-away party for us, since in a few more days we'll be setting sail on Dolphin Dreamer for the Bahamas.

It will be hard to say good-bye to the friends we've made on Cedar Key — both dolphin and human! — but it is good to know that Rosie is safely home again, and, with the help of Gavin Davis, the future of CETA seems secure.

You will find lots more about dolphins on these web-sites:

The Whale and Dolphin Conservation Society
www.wdcs.org

International Dolphin Watch
www.idw.org